Previously published books about the adventures of the Flowers' family include "Goldie's Garden".

Ken Olive is currently working on the next in this Flowers series.

Also look for thrillers written by Ken Olive under the nom de plume, Robert Lester. A mystery thriller being released this winter.

Special Corps

Personal Protection

A Flowers' Book...by Ken Olive

To Pam. For putting up with me for 34 years. For better or worse, in sickness or in health.

Publisher: Ken Olive Publishing

ISBN-13: 978-0-615-40404-2
ISBN-10: 0-615-40404-9

First Edition: September 2010

10 9 8 7 6 5 4 3 2 1

Brothers

Rising rap singer, "Willie Delicious", finished his high energy performance at the Mississippi Coast Coliseum in front of a thunderous, raucous audience. They had been warmed up by the opening act, "Gangsta Group", perfect for the crowd. They were good enough to be entertaining, but wouldn't overshadow the main "headliner."

What the audience didn't know, however, was that warm-up group was actually led by Willie's younger brother, LaTrelle. Both of their "legal" last names were Johnson, but they never used that...too common, Willie said. Too "white" LaTrelle insisted. Willie thought he was helping his brother get into the business. LaTrelle felt like Willie was holding him back. The resentment had been building for months.

LaTrelle felt he was a much better entertainer, and was tired of taking the "leftovers" from Willie. Tonight he would make things "righteous", he vowed. After the show, LaTrelle and two of his "posse" waited in a dark corner of the parking lot, right behind Willie's Escalade. LaTrelle's boys both had Glocks, the 9mm variety, stuck into their pants.

"Here he comes," said Harris, the larger of the two assassins. "Let him get closer," LaTrelle said. Willie and the lead guitar of the group strode toward the Cadillac. As they approached to about 20 feet, two men positioned behind LaTrelle, grabbed the men with the Glocks in choke holds, and one of them pointed a 9mm Beretta at LaTrelle, "Don't do a thing," said the man. Simultaneously, a silver Range Rover screeched to a stop between the approaching Willie, and the Escalade.

Josh's radio crackled, "All OK ", as they disarmed, and pushed the three would-be killers out into the light. Josh Flowers got out of the SUV and watched as his men put "flex-cuffs" on the three of them.

Willie smirked, "I told the white boy here he was crazy, that we was brothers. He told me if he was wrong, he would apologize. I s'pose he wasn't wrong, was he little brother?"

LaTrelle said, "You got it all wrong, bro." "Don't look that way to me," Willie came back. Josh looked at his #2 man, Kenyon White, and asked, "Police on the way?" "Affirmative" Kenyon replied.

"What's with that? We didn't do nothin," LaTrelle shouted.

"Your boys have State issued permits for those two Glocks?" Josh asked. The men looked at the ground. "I didn't think so, but we do for ours," Josh pointed out. "You'll all three be taking a short ride down to the jailhouse." LaTrelle said, "I didn't have no gun." "Well, you might get off then," said Josh. "It's not up to me."

"Yeah, little brother, you might get off from the man, but not from me." Willie smiled. LaTrelle answered in a cocky manner, "We'll just see, this ain't over."

Just then, two patrol cars pulled up, and after a short discussion, took the men into custody. A big cop named Pitalo looked at the men and asked, "Harris, when did they let you out of Parchman?", and they drove off.

"Could be a long night for Harris," Josh noted. "Coulda been a short night for me," Willie said, "I owe you man." "Josh disagreed, "You already paid me what you owed me. But, a referral or two for 'Special Corps' wouldn't hurt my feelings." "You got it, J, no problem."

"Well we have to get a new opener for tomorrow night. Lucky there's lots of available talent always hanging around." Willie said.

"Kenyon and Julio will make sure you get back to the hotel, and we've got two men assigned there, right next door at the 'Hard Rock', for the duration," Josh explained.

"We cool, man, thanks again," Willie said as he walked toward the Escalade. Josh stopped him.

"Let me check it out, first." Josh went through the glove compartment, storage unit in the front seat, under the seats, then jammed his hand under the passenger seat cushion.

"Look what I found," Josh said holding up a bag of white powder. "That ain't mine, you know how I feel about that shit, man," Willie declared. "I believe you," Josh replied. "This was planted so the police would figure the shooting was 'drug related', and wouldn't dig around too much for the truth."

"Also, I'm sure the police will be getting an anonymous tip later tonight about 'your' stash. This was insurance, in case the hit didn't happen. I'll take it and flush it," Josh stated. "I have no idea what it is, could be talcum powder. I'm not committing a crime."

"My own brother," Willie kept muttering to himself, "My own brother," as he drove away with Josh's men tailing right behind.

On cue, at 2 am, two Biloxi Police officers knocked on Willie's door with a search warrant for the Escalade. Willie went to the parking garage with them, opened the door, and stood back, with a big smile.

The first place they looked was under the passenger seat cushion. Then, 30 minutes later they thanked Willie for his cooperation, and returned to their "snitch" at the jail. It was going to be a long night for someone.

Background

My name is Josh Flowers. I'm 23 years old, I live in Biloxi, Mississippi. This is a town considered to be part of a region called the Mississippi Gulf Coast. About 150,000 people live in nine or ten communities with shared borders. The region is almost equidistant between New Orleans and Mobile, about 60 miles east and west. In the past few years, Biloxi has become one of the largest casino gaming towns in the United States.

I am the owner of a personal security business named "Special Corps". I started the company after a 2-year stint in a little tropical paradise called Afghanistan. I was a U.S. Marine sergeant there, but was put on my present course by an AK-47 round which shattered my femur. Now I've had some body work done, and while the new hip doesn't slow me down, it disqualified me from further duty to my beloved Marine Corps.

I founded this company over 2 years ago. With the 50-odd casinos, boxing matches, and entertainers coming through here, there's plenty of work to do, and we're the best. My first hire was Kenyon White, an ex-Navy SEAL, 25 years old, and smart as they come.

My next hire was his polar opposite, except for the smarts, Milo Stewart, who is the biggest computer geek, hacker, and "know it all", since Bill Gates. Milo also dates one of my sisters, Jess, but that not why he got the job. I have 2 other employees, a former "Green Beret", named Julio, and a man mountain we call "Half Track". In busy times we can add some temporary staff, who I trust.

We made it through Hurricane Katrina, 20 months ago. There was a lot of human suffering, but, as far as most of the Gulf Coast was concerned, the storm the had unintended side effect of clearing more land for casinos to be built, and gave a fledgling security company a "jump start." Everybody wanted security. We were busy, but we never took on more than we could handle.

Despite lucrative offers from New Orleans businesses, 60 miles west, we stayed here. This is where my family lives, and this is where the company wants to be. To wander off for a quick buck was tempting, but we're rooted here.

The Gulf Coast has seen destruction like this many times before. Hurricane Betsey, September 1965, 155 mph winds, Hurricane Camille, 1969, gusts up to 220 mph, sustained winds at 190 mph. But, just as in the past, the citizens here banded together and rebuilt. There was no looting, no crying about entitlement, just hard work. Today, you'd be hard pressed to find evidence of Katrina damage on the Mississippi coast.

The population, here, is very diverse. The seafood industry was the largest employer here for decades. Immigrants from Greece, Italy, Slovakia, Viet Nam, work side by side with the whites, blacks, and Cajuns. Everybody who wanted a job, usually had two of them.

My Mom and Dad live here. My Dad, Tom, retired from the Air Force when his unit was deactivated, and is now the VP of Human Resources at the huge "Beau Rivage" hotel/casino complex. The casino owners, MGM Resorts International, have several similar properties, such as the "Bellagio" in Las Vegas.

Karen, my Mom, was a librarian for awhile, but now tends her garden full-time, only filling in at the library in emergencies.

I have two sisters. Connie is a real estate agent. My parents adopted her when Connie's mother (my Mom's sister) suddenly died of an aneurism, a couple of years ago. My Grandma also moved in with us after the funeral.

She and Connie had lived with my aunt Vicky in San Antonio. My other sister, Jess, has graduated culinary/hotel management school, and is in the management training program, at the "Beau Rivage". Our Dad's boss hired her strictly on grades and ability, not favoritism. He also makes sure she works the hours, no one else wants to work.

My Grandma, Doris, now lives with her boy friend Max Bergeron. More on them later. We also have a 2-year old yellow Labrador retriever. She came to us mysteriously, just a week after we had lost a very special yellow Labrador retriever. That special Lab had rescued Jess from a hurricane, Connie from an attacker, and saved Doris' life when she drunkenly fell and cut herself badly. We decided to name the new pup "Goldie," just like her predecessor. It was not only to honor our late family member, but my Mom almost believes that the new Lab, is a reincarnation of the former one. Jess still had her cat, Princess, who was starting to show her age.

The family has a tradition of getting everyone together for dinner, each Sunday at noon. About 90% of the time we succeed.

You'll learn more about everyone later...this is just the beginning.

The Fighter

Two days after the parking lot showdown between Willie and his brother, Kenyon and I drove Willie to the airport, where he was taking a private plane to Atlanta. He had a big show scheduled there. I like what my personal sendoff represents. The owner of the company shows respect, and extra service to the client. It gives me an edge the next time he needs help, and when he refers me. "Hey man, thanks for being on top of things, including the car and the baggie," Willie reminded me.

We have a competitor in the area, aptly named "Viper Security." They use tactics which are less than above-board, with their clients, and their competitors. They'll cut fees, (services accordingly), and they try to steal our employees and clients. They'll also let the client dictate operations, which caused them an embarrassing incident last year. In this business, one failure can ruin your credibility.

This trip to the airport was not totally focused on Willie. Once he passed through TSA security, our job was done. We had another client coming in 90 minutes later. This would be the welterweight contender Hector "The Victor" Ruiz. He would be coming in on another leased plane, with his entourage, for a fight two nights from now at The "Beau Rivage".

Kenyon and I had driven to Houston for a presentation, last month. Our job would be guaranteeing his safety from the time he reached the airport, through tomorrow's press conference, the fight itself, and our job would end when he left the airport three days hence.

At our meeting, we voiced our standing policy. That is, we were being paid to provide protection for Hector, only, not his trainer, manager, cut man, or any of a dozen parasites who latch onto fighters and entertainers.

As always, we would be paid by certified check no later than 10 days prior to the job.

This caused some consternation with his business manager, Raul, who said that we would be paid from the gate proceeds. Even at my age, I've seen enough of those old movies to know that they "cook the books" in the fight game. During our negotiation Kenyon spoke up about our policies.

"I was a Green Beret for 7 years, and won three, field combat medals. My boss over there, is one of the most highly decorated Marines, ever," he said, nodding toward me.

Kenyon continued "He was nominated for the Congressional Medal of Honor, for extreme valor under fire. Thanks, but we don't need the practice." We prepared to leave, and Hector nodded to his manager. "Pay them," he said.

I knew that this was the "tune up" fight in Hector's try for the "belt". The last thing he wanted was to be worried about his safety. Obviously, he trusted us with the job.

Now at the airport, we waited inside the terminal where the private planes unloaded. Our wait was rewarded in about an hour, when a big Lear Jet squealed it's tires on the tarmac.

"We're on," I said, and we walked over to the closest, unsecured area possible. Hector deplaned from probably a 45 minute flight, and headed straight for us, once we got his attention. He had a beautiful, young woman with him, he introduced her as "Rosita". Hector said, "The others handle the bags, we will come with you."

I asked him to come with me a few feet from the others. I didn't want to get started off on the wrong foot. Entertainers all had machismo, chutzpah, balls, or whatever, and didn't like to be lectured to or shown up in front of the "help." "She's not part of the deal," I said. "She is with me," replied Hector, "Where I go, she goes."

Josh explained, "You have a choice to make, Hector. Either our fee goes up 25%, and I'm being generous here, or if there's any danger, she's dead weight, we leave her behind...our job is to protect you only." He thought a second and decided, "OK, any trouble, she's on her own."

Our plan was simple. Two of us would stay in the suite with Hector, at all times. Our back-up and relief would be in an identical suite across the hall. We had the usual hotel security. They were good at breaking up fights, and noisy parties, but for life-threatening incidents, they were no help.

Hector and Rosita rode with us. A second car containing Julio and Half Track would be trailing two cars behind us.

We entered through a private doorway at the "Beau Rivage". Hector had been preregistered in his suite, and we had the another suite across the hall for our team. On the way up, we switched room keys, in case of a leak. We planned on moving him again the day before the fight. Everyone got settled in.

After about an hour, there was a knock at the door. It was Hector's business manager. I walked to Hector's room and knocked lightly. He answered "Por que?" I said, "It's Raul at the door. Are you expecting him?" "It's OK," he answered.

I let Raul in, and he walked into the room, right between the portable metal detectors we had hidden on each side of the door. He wasn't carrying. Hector sent Rosita out to us. I figured he could handle himself with Raul, but took nothing for granted. We stayed out of normal earshot, but we could hear a struggle, if one occurred.

Later, room service brought dinner to the original suite where Hector was booked. We wheeled it across the hall for Hector and Rosita. A steak and potatoes for Hector, weigh-in was yesterday, in Houston. Welterweight class was under 147 pounds, but Hector only needed to make that number, or less, at the weigh-in. He would probably weigh at least 10 pounds more at fight time, which was common for all weight classes. Rosita had a salad. Kenyon and I would eat when we were relieved for the evening.

This morning was the always-eventful press conference. Hector and his opponent, a young black kid named Jimmy "The Killer" Miller, would pose, talk trash, and carry on like they wanted to start the fight early. Hector told me, "He's going to come at me, try to throw a sucker punch." That's what Raul and Jimmy's manager had concocted, thus the visit by Raul yesterday.

Hector continued, "Whatever you do, don't hurt him, I need this fight," he said. I told him that I was out of the stage show, he could let his "hangers on" break up the fight. I would only intervene if it got out of hand or if Hector called on me.

The press was assembled in a large conference room at the hotel, when we walked in with Hector. Of course, for effect and theatrics, the lower ranked man was awaiting Hector on the dais. There were the usual dull and boring questions. Finally, a reporter asked Jimmy if he had respect for Hector's accomplishments.

Jimmy said, "Yeah, just one, he banging that 'puta' over there" pointing at Rosita. "How about you pay me a little visit tonight senorita...I'll show you what a real man is like, not this 'candy ass' boy, but a real man, that's what you need. I'm surprised he showed up at all. Guess he was late getting here 'cause he had to work up the nerve to face me."

Needless to say, all hell broke loose. Calling out Hector's woman and questioning his virility, were too much to take, especially on tape, and in front of a crowd. Hector leapt on the table and started wading through people toward Jimmy.

His handlers couldn't control him. "Chinga tu Madre" Hector yelled in Spanish, "Tu morte, esse." People were falling off the table, Hector was kicking at the arms of people who were trying to grab him. Jimmy was pretending to be held back. Hector wasn't pretending. I yelled to Half Track, "Get Rosita off the stage, back to the room."

I looked at Kenyon, he nodded and we wedged our way toward Hector.

Kenyon, all 6'3", 235 pounds of him, with almost no body fat grabbed Hector around the chest, pinning his arms to his sides. Me, just 6'1" and 185 with a hip replacement, secured Hector's legs, and we pulled him off the stage and carried him to his elevator, Hector was kicking and screaming.

We got him into his suite, and he was still spitting Spanish curses at Jimmy, and, I'm sure, at us. "Put me down, esse!" He glared at me. Kenyon and I put him on the couch, I'd had enough machismo for today.

"Shut up," I screamed. "Do you have any idea how much money we saved you just now?"

"What if you'd slipped off the table and broken your foot, or worse, your arm? Where would you be then? You said you needed this fight. Tell me. What would an injury cost you?"

"Millions," I answered. "We protected you from the possibility of losing millions, that's how much," I said. "Not just this fight, but the championship, fight, then your title defense."

I ranted, "Pay per view, *HBO*, *Sports Center*, would be lost, all for macho pride. You have to think these things through."

About that time Julio and Half Track entered the room with a flustered Rosita. I pointed at her, "You defended your woman. You were right to do so. I just couldn't let you get yourself hurt and lose everything over anger. You'll take care of Jimmy in the ring. You'll make him pay, but the right way."

Hector had calmed down. He took a Corona out of the mini bar and went in the bedroom, Rosita was crying.

He came out in 10 minutes and pulled me to the corner. "OK, man" he said, "you saved me from myself. Rosita said it too." He held me close and whispered, "An extra 25% for her, too. I'll call Raul right now, you'll have a check in an hour." He went back to the bedroom. Overall, I was satisfied with our execution.

But, now we had to split our attention between two people. It wasn't just Hector, anymore. Where was the "sucker punch" I wondered?

My cell phone was vibrating. It was Dad. "Mr. Tom Flowers" in front of his peers, but right now, just Dad. "Hey, I saw you on our monitors," he chided. "That hip looked OK, do you want a tape for replay?" he laughed.

Of course I knew, you couldn't go to the bathroom in a casino without being filmed. "No Dad, Kenyon would just use it to ask for a raise."

"How's Mom doing since I saw her last week. Is she worried about the pre-fight activity?" I asked.

"I doubt that she knows anything about it. But the girls will tell her the details of the side-show," his Dad warned.

Tom continued, "And you know her and that garden, it's almost a half acre, now, and Goldie II is still the perfect image of Goldie I. I'm telling you, that dog knows things, it's weird."

"Well, Dad, the fight is Friday night, Hector will leave Saturday, I'll be over for dinner at noon on Sunday." "Karen will love hearing that, everyone else too." We hung up, and I rejoined the crew, repeating the plan.

"OK," I said, "one hour and we switch rooms. We had them deliver a late lunch to this room today, even let them have a little glimpse of Hector. Anyone on the staff will think he's in this room. Hector knows we're swapping rooms. I had someone I trust, move their clothes during the press conference."

"This should be just by the numbers." I said. "We do the switch, quick, and clean. Swap the metal detector, reset the posts, and bingo, we're set."

When it was time, I knocked lightly on Hector's door. He and Rosita were ready. I looked out into the hall, the door to both suites were open, they walked the 8 feet across the hall, like clockwork. "Por que?" Hector asked again. "Better to be safe..." I said.

Really, there was no translation needed. Kenyon and I took the first watch. Julio and "Track" would take the next, at 8 pm. At 7pm, we pulled the dinner switch again.

The Main Event

Finally it was "Fight Night" at the casino. Getting Hector to the ring was easy. Back hallways, security doors, and restricted access areas were the route to the dressing rooms. My larger concern was while he was in the ring.

One only had to remember the Monica Seles stabbing during a tennis match in 1993. Having won 7 of the previous "Grand Slam" events, a maniac who was enamored with Steffi Graf, stabbed and tried to kill Seles during a match in Hamburg. It ended Seles career. No one was ready to protect the athletes.

Josh delivered Hector to the ring without incident. Hector has morphed into his "Hector The Victor", role which was required stagemanship. Kenyon and I sat in the 5th row, across the ring from each other. I would scan his side and my right, he would reciprocate. Julio and "Track" were milling through the room with "Fight Nite" t-shirts on. The hotel didn't have size XXXXL for "Track", so they sewed two XXL shirts together. It turned out to show "Fight NiFightNite", but who reads those things anyway?

The Mayor of Biloxi had the honor of introducing the contestants. He yelled "Let's Get Ready to Get It On" and the fight was on. It was mercifully short. Hector knocked his man down twice in the 2nd, and the fight was declared a TKO, Hector winning, in the third round. We hustled Hector out of the ring, back to his dressing room. No such luck for Jimmy. Many of those who paid big money for their seats, felt cheated, like Jimmy had "taken a dive" and were advancing to the stage. I noticed my rival, Butch Wingo, of "Viper", in the ring kicking some people who were trying to get at Jimmy. "Look back there," I shouted to Hector. "Jimmy's protected by Viper," I added. "Vaya con Dios," Hector said, making the sign of the cross.

The next morning, Kenyon and I would take Hector to the Airport. Tonight, we still had a job to do. You can have a "let down" after a big event like this.

We had to stay alert until we said our goodbyes to him and Rosita, at the airport tomorrow. After that, I had given the men the rest of the weekend off, plus Monday and Tuesday. We had a big new job coming up in 10 days, and we would start planning next Wednesday.

But tonight we had to remain diligent. At 9:45 there was a knock on the door. I looked through the peephole, and then stood to the side of the door. "Who is it?" I said. "Fruit basket from the management for Mr. Ruiz." I thought for a moment.

Well, this was the room he was initially booked into, I thought. "OK," I said, "leave it outside." "You have to sign for the basket," the man said." "Who is the general manager of the hotel?" I asked. "Mr. Rutland," he answered. He was right. I looked out again, he didn't look like a bad guy.

I nodded to Kenyon, he moved to his right. We would have the guy between us. I opened the door, the man smiled, took half a step, and stared at Kenyon pointing a Mossberg 12 gauge, "Persuader" model right at his stomach. "Still want me to sign?" I asked. "Nn.nn.no sir, I'll leave the basket on the floor here."

He passed through the metal detector and it's LED turned red. "What are you carrying?", I asked. He was frozen. "What are you carrying?" I asked again. You could see him thinking, as he was looking at the red light. "My radio?" he said. We checked him out, he didn't have a weapon. I took out my cell and called Mr. Flowers, and he ID'd the guy as a 5-year employee. False alarm, this time. But, we had been on top of the situation. The man left the suite...he was shaking.

Hector had heard the discussion, and came outside his room, after the clerk left. "You did good, Hector, always wait until it's over." "No, you two did good," he added "that guy was not going to get to me, I felt really safe. What's that smell?" he was saying, as he went to tell Rosita the coast was clear.

I knew Dad would be buying the clerk a new pair of pants and billing me, if the clerk took the chance of mentioning the incident and literally, becoming the "butt" of some very bad jokes from his co-workers.

Saturday, the airport trip was easy, and we waved as Hector and Rosita entered the secure area. Another happy client!

Sunday Dinner

I arrived for the traditional Flowers' Sunday dinner a little early, at 10:30, dinner was at noon. I wanted to visit with the family, including Goldie II, the 2-year old yellow Lab. She had mysteriously come into our lives only a week after her namesake, Goldie, had been euthanized due to terminal cancer. We held on to her for as long as we could, but when the pain became the dominate force in her life, we didn't let her suffer any longer.

Then, after work, a week later, on his way home from work, Dad found this little yellow pup in the middle of the road. We adopted her instantly. Mom thinks the dog was a gift from heaven, who adopted us. Maybe she's right.

After hugging my parents, I went into the kitchen where my sisters, Connie and Jess, were preparing dinner. Jess had graduated culinary/hotel management school a few months ago, and was now in charge of the weekly event.

Connie was about to enter her 3rd year of residential real estate, and was progressing and earning some money, after the usual beginning struggle. She had turned from a "wild child" into an energy filled young person, right before my eyes. Connie was learning her way around the kitchen under Jess's tutelage. She would help clean up afterwards, and 3 out of 4 weeks, she had an "open house" from 2pm to 4pm.

I gave the girls a big hug, and shared some small talk with them for a few minutes.

I took a walk outside, with Goldie (II) following dinner as usual. My family lived about 20 minutes north of the casino strip and highway 90. They were north, across the Biloxi Back Bay, in an area of town called De'Iberville. It was more rural here, and that suited Dad just fine. They owned 5 acres which extended on a peninsula down to the bay waters where Dad had a small "John" boat tied to a dock. He wasn't an avid fisherman, but it gave him an escape from the "hustle & bustle" of the casino where he worked. The 5 acres provided Mom with plenty of room for her expanding garden.

This property was as far as you could get from the ever-pulsating "strip", with non-stop casinos. That's why Dad had picked this place. It was peaceful.

I walked down to the dock with Goldie. It was sort of my little escape too. After about 30 minutes of peace, I saw a gold colored, 30-year old, Lincoln Town Car, including whitewalls, pull up in the oyster shell driveway. Grandma, and her boy friend, Max had arrived.

"Time to face the music," I said to Goldie. "I can't let them suffer alone." Goldie sort of let out a little whine, but followed me inside.

Max and Grandma Doris entered the front door. Max was dressed in yellow "sans-a-belt" double-knit slacks, an orange checked shirt, electric blue bow tie, and "the full Cleveland", white patent shoes and belt. Grandma had on a sundress and had absolutely bathed herself in a foul-smelling perfume.

"I'm going to the screened porch to smoke my stogie", she announced, everyone immediately agreeing on her idea. She had a small trip on the rug in the entrance, and everybody knew that she had already been having her wine.

As she would often say in a paraphrase of an old "Gallo Brothers" commercial, "I will drink no wine, before it's time", and then add, "And it's always time."

We had a wonderful dinner with Cornish game hens, early potatoes, green salad, and bread. This all came naturally to

Jess, who was more at home with her kitchen, than with Milo, her "off and on" boy friend.

After a great dinner, plus peach cobbler for dessert, the men, and Goldie, retired to the family room, and the Braves game. This was not my favorite time of year, but until football started next month, this was it. Then we could start cheering for the Saints.

"So, what's new?" I asked my sisters, before going to watch the baseball game. "Why don't you tell us?" Connie responded gleefully. "I saw you on TV at the fight press conference."

"It's all an act," I said, not to worry them, but I knew that's "usually" the case. It was just a little "white lie." Jess jumped in, "It sure didn't look like an act, there were more "bleeps" on *Sports Center* than actual words." So we made cable sports TV, I thought. Not bad.

"Well," I said, "They use pre-fights to increase the gate. It was nothing really."

Dad reminded me, "I think you owe me a pair of pants for one of my employees." We laughed and I said, " Yeah, guess I do." The girls looked at Dad with puzzled expressions. "Just part of the business," he said, "I'll never tell."

"Who are you working with next?" Mom asked. I hesitated, "Holly Santa Cruz," I answered. This unleashed an outburst of squeals from the 2 girls. "No way," Connie said with eyes like saucers. "Way," I said in return. "Can we meet her, can we get her autograph, can we be backstage?" They were both saying at once. "She's at the "Beau Rivage" for 2 nights, you'll have to ask Dad," I said. "You know I don't mix business with personal."

"You're ungrateful," Jess teased. "I move Hector Ruiz's clothes during the press conference for you, cook you a great meal, and you deny your two sisters a favor?"

"Yeah, sorry, I forgot to thank you for moving their stuff. I owe you. But this I cannot do. She's 'BIG TIME', and could be a major asset to my company."

"But Josh," Connie pleaded, "she's bigger than Madonna." "Exactly," I said, "exactly." "Now, I've got to go. She'll be here a week from this Wednesday, perform Thursday and Friday, then be off to Vegas and the Bellagio."

"Hopefully, I'll see you guys next week. Say goodbye to all the sleeping angels for me. Grandma too," I laughed.

Holly

Holly Santa Cruz (actually, Holly Canfield), at age 24, was the biggest song and music video star in the western hemisphere, and she knew it. I was referred to her by her Father, who was a retired Marine Colonel I had met. He had liked me from the beginning of my tour of duty in Afghanistan. Connections never hurt.

Kenyon and I had driven to meet her in New Orleans, while she was doing a benefit for Katrina victims, about 6 months ago. We weren't involved in the security there, but she was already booked at the "Beau Rivage" for two nights this summer, so we took the opportunity for a meeting.

I knew they could do things in videos and on TV to enhance one's appearance, but this girl was naturally hot! She knew that too, the way she slid her tiny skirt up another couple of inches, anytime she was talking to a man. About 5' 5", 110 pounds, I guessed, and all of it put in exactly the right places. Copper shaded red hair and green eyes, wow! Fortunately, her Dad had accompanied her, as he was organizing military and ex-military volunteers on special hurricane relief projects in the 9th ward.

Colonel Canfield was about as "no-nonsense" as anyone could be. "My little girl here, he nodded at Holly, is going through a rough patch. You've probably read about the divorce." (she was splitting with a country singer named Billy Wade Monroe. No kids, thankfully, but it was ugly).

"Yes sir, we have," Kenyon said with me nodding. Part of our job was to put each client's life, and close acquaintances under a microscope, and assess any threats we found.

The Colonel continued, "Well, he's not a happy boy, and things

things may get ugly. He's prone to violence. He beat his last wife so bad she spent a week in the hospital, then she refused to press charges. What makes a man like that?" The Colonel just shook his head and looked at the floor.

"And, Col. Canfield continued, "he's from Houston, just a few miles down the road. He has lots of friends there." "We're aware of Mr. Monroe's reputation," I replied.

"Well, I had someone look through your file, Flowers, yours too White, no offense meant." "None taken, Sir," we replied simultaneously.

"Well, dammit, it's my daughter. But, you both passed muster easily, or you wouldn't be here. Enough medals and commendations between you two to cover the entire Italian Army." "Thank you, Sir," I repeated. "I think we both saw that as serving our country."

"I've said my piece, and done my homework. I'll just sit quietly, and let Holly talk to you. She's her own person, her Mother and I raised her to be that."

We both turned our attention to the young woman sitting across from us, and waited for her to begin.

"I want to know what you provide, when you start and finish, and how much this is going to cost?" She detailed her entourage, "I travel with a group, as do most entertainers. These include my hairdressers, makeup artist, masseuse, wardrobe expert, and personal bodyguard, my friend Clete."

"Also," she said, "there is a second group of sound and show experts, the band, people from my studio, special effects people, etc., they usually arrive earlier than I, to do the setup. So exactly what do you do?"

I looked at Kenyon, and I began. "We protect your safety, yours alone, from the time you exit the secure space at the airport, until you clear security on the way out."

I added, "We protect you at the hotel, during rehearsals, meals, during the show, and afterwards. We do not protect anyone else who is with you, unless we are paid extra to do so, and that includes Clete. He can be around you all he wants, but unarmed." She raised her eyebrows. "If he has a weapon on him, we will disarm him."

Then the kicker, "And if that weapon isn't registered in Mississippi, we'll have him arrested. That's what we do."

I continued, "Our methods are of no importance to you, we guarantee your safety, period. Once you get to your penthouse suite, we will be in the room at all times, with back-up less than 60 seconds away. We have our travel, and yes, escape routes down, and constantly change them at random." I could see her Father nodding, out of the corner of my eye.

Lastly, "Our fee for stepping in front of a bullet or knife meant for you is $25,000." She looked shocked. I finished, "Per day, or partial day. In your case $75,000 by cashiers check in our hands no later than 10 days prior to the commencement of the job." I asked, "Do you have any other questions?" "Well, Clete is going to be around, and he loves his pistol and a little derringer he carries in his boot. He says it makes us safer," she countered.

"Absolutely not," I said, "He's an amateur, no offense, but I can't sing or dance...I don't try to something I can't do! Plus, I'm sure he's not authorized to carry a gun in my state. If we get into a 'situation', I don't know how he will respond. I know how my men react, he'd be more harm than good. I know the roadways, the area, and the hotel security, he doesn't."

She thought about it for a moment. Holly got up and walked gracefully (concentrate, Josh), into the next room. She returned with a 30ish man all decked out in "bling" a passenger on the gravy train, hoping it never stopped.

Kenyon and I stared a hole through a man we suspected was Clete. I started in, "I assume you heard the conversation," I said. It wasn't a question. "Yeah, I did," Clete confessed. "I'm OK with it. Anything that will make Holly more safe," he added. "And no interference?" I stated. "None," Clete affirmed.

"Anything further from us, I asked?" "No," she said. "you're top of the line pros, like my Dad told me. You'll have your signed contract and your check, in a week."

We thanked them and left. In the hall I told Kenyon, "We'll bring Drake and Pete in for this job." Drake and Pete were two pros, who had their own small security company. We had discussed a merger, but they wanted their own shop. They would work on a contract basis with us, when we had a big job like Holly.

The Cake !

It was another Sunday traditional family dinner day at the Flowers' home. This particular weekend we were also celebrating the birthday of Grandma Doris (age unrevealed). She loved being the center of attention, so everyone promised Karen that they would try to make the day as special as possible for Doris.

She and her boyfriend Max arrived at noon, Max was resplendent in yellow double-knit pants, red tropical shirt adorned with green and blue parrots, and the full Cleveland, white patent shoes and belt. Doris had on her frilly, low cut, blue dress, with shoes the same color as Max's. Her hair had just been done in a style that used to be called a "bee hive" decades ago.

Grandma was also wearing an aroma which was a strange mix of cheroot cigarillo, sweet perfume, and red wine. She actually had an old red wine spot on the back of her dress...how had that happened?

Doris had announced that after we had dinner and her celebration (meaning wine and toasting), that she and Max would head over to Saint Helena's Senior Center, for a celebration with a few of their friends. After all, she said "I want to celebrate with some of our older friends as well, just not Betty Malbon," who Grandma Doris had a running feud with.

Jess had prepared her Grandmother's birthday dinner with all Doris' favorites. Veal chops (Goldie loved the bones), baby red potatoes, green beans, all served after a fresh salad.

Dessert was a German chocolate cake, topped by one, lone candle. Jess stuck her head out of the kitchen and said, "Dinner will be ready in ten minutes. You've been warned."

"Great," exclaimed Doris, "let's open the wine." Tom and Karen looked at each other, with a small shake of the head, and Tom went to the cabinet to get a bottle of cabernet sauvignon which had been highly recommended by the owner of a small wine shop in Biloxi.

It was a special occasion, and he wanted to treat it like one. Tom knew that Karen always tried to make the best of such celebrations, despite her Mom's erratic behavior. "We're going to need more than that, Tommy boy," Doris shouted. He did a "U" turn and came back with two bottles.

"That's more like it," she assured him. Dad opened the first bottle and Doris held up her glass right away, "Birthday girl first, and don't be shy with the pour."

A few minutes later Jess and Connie served dinner, starting with Grandma, of course. It was great, everyone agreed, and Tom wound up opening a third bottle of wine.

The birthday cake arrived at the table with fanfare, and was gloriously adorned with "Happy Birthday Grandma", written in white chocolate icing, and the one candle. It took Doris three tries to blow out the candle, but she did it and then announced to the group in slurred speech that she had wished for a "Max"imum ride, later that night from her "big boy."

Everybody blushed, especially Max, and they tried to ignore her comment and change the subject. Doris was really getting into the "spirit" of her special day. However, Karen didn't like Doris having a knife in her hand when she was already tipsy, so she cut the cake, presenting her mother with the first piece. Doris gobbled her cake and washed it down with some more wine. She then adjourned to the back porch, to smoke her "stogie."

Max tried to apologize for Doris, but everyone assured him that Doris was just being Doris, and that's just the way things were in her world.

Josh and his Dad cleared the table, trying hard to appear as modern, helpful, men, and then went into the family room, along with Goldie tagging along, to watch sports on TV. This was their escape from what had already been a bizarre birthday dinner.

They had their entertainment for the day, now was time for a ball game. They had invited Max to sit with them, and he did for a while. Tom knew that Max probably deserved a break from Doris, which Max appreciated.

In about thirty minutes, Max stood and announced that it was time for them to get over to the Senior Center, and he went to the back porch to collect Doris. Karen had just begun to let Goldie outside, so she and Max entered the porch at about the same time.

"What's that smell," Karen asked, not really expecting an answer. The answer was self evident. Doris had passed out and her "stogie" had burned a inch deep, round hole right on the side of her hairdo. The cigar was still burning, but was now safely on the cement floor of the screened porch, almost out.

"Oh God," Karen exclaimed, and with that Doris came out of her stupor, downing the last of the wine from her glass. "Well, sorry folks," she said, "but it's time for me to go see my friends at the Center."

She pushed herself out of the chair, and wobbled off through the house toward the front door. Max and Karen stood there in stunned disbelief.

Doris looked back and asked, "Isn't somebody going to open the door for the b<u>urf</u>day gal?" Max hurried along, and they were gone in a flash. Tom came in and asked his wife why she looked so pale. Karen answered, "I should be used to it by now. Why am I ever surprised?"

The next stop was the Senior Center, and her friends had decided to play a trick on Doris. Everyone was going to act like they had forgotten about her birthday, and then after ten minutes or so Sammy Pantolino was going to wheel in a three-layered coconut cake, again with only one candle.

It would be a surprise. Max knew about the ruse, but had promised to keep it from Doris. He figured she would be happy they had done something extra special for her.

Max had purposefully stayed sober so that he could drive on this day. He traveled slowly down the road with Doris complaining that she wanted him to go faster. Her friends were waiting, after all.

They pulled up into the parking area and once Max had parked, Doris got a bottle of red wine out of the trunk and poured herself some for herself, into a plastic glass she kept there. She couldn't, by law, have an open bottle inside the car, so this was her adaptation. She screwed the cap back on and brought the bottle inside with her.

Once they entered the Center, everyone was off in their own little groups, chatting, playing bridge, checkers and the like. Everyone was ignoring Doris. She couldn't figure it out.

Doris walked through the room and people said "hi" and nodded, but nothing special. Nothing which made Doris the center of attention, anyway. Suddenly, Doris spotted Betty Malbon in the corner of the room, obviously trying to lure in husband #4. "What's she doing here?" Doris demanded. Max said, "It's a free country, she comes here all the time."

"Well, I don't like her here on my birthday," said Doris, as she poured herself another glass of wine. They sat down in a pre-arranged space in the middle of the room, this was the signal.

Sammy came out of the kitchen area wheeling a cake large enough to feed 50 people, and all the seniors turned to the center of the room and began to sing, "Happy birthday to Doris..." Doris was loving it. Everyone came over and started hugging her.

They lit the candle and Doris got up from her seat to blow it out, but she stumbled. She tried to use the cart to steady herself, but it was on wheels. Doris fell on Mildred Weaver and the cart flew 6 feet in Max's direction, the cake sliding off the cart when it hit Max, landing upside down in his lap.

Doris was confused, the room was spinning. She was only sober enough to see Betty Malbon cleaning the cake off of Max's pants, but she was too drunk to do anything about it.

The commotion settled down, and Max said, "Sorry, she's been feeling poorly all day. She only came out because she wanted to be with her friends," he finished. Max and Sammy helped the old woman to the car, and Max drove her home to sleep it off. A birthday to remember.

A Few Days Off

My place is a nice little 2-bedrooom flat on the third floor of a small condominium complex, about 500 yards from the Gulf of Mexico, just off Beauvoir Road.

Connie had helped me find it, and I used the V.A. Benefits of almost no down payment, to purchase it. I could have paid cash. I had enough saved from my combat duty pay (read "tax free"), to buy it outright. But, I was conservative, and always wanted to have a reserve fund. Something in the bank for a rainy day, my Dad would always say. Being self-employed, I always worried plenty about risk, to make me cautious. But, this place was special.

My furnishings, appointments, kitchen, and décor was simple and comfortable. I liked things that way. I didn't have expensive art hanging on the walls, just some prints and reproductions which I thought looked nice. I only splurged on things which were useful to my work, like laptops, a "Blackberry", and my Range Rover. Plus, I had the condo, with great, keep to themselves, neighbors. I had Mr. Levy and his second wife, Belle, on one side of me, and a widow, Ms. Cook, on the other.

Nightly breezes off the Gulf were welcome. I had a small lanai off the back deck with a table and chairs, where I could sip a Corona and gather my thoughts. This location was only about 10 minutes from the Biloxi "strip" crammed in with hotels, casinos, and restaurants...but it really seemed like a different world.

My small business office was in a non-descript little 1-story brick complex, 10 minutes north off "Popp's Ferry Road." We didn't want to advertise who we were to the whole world.

The sign over the door simply said S.C., LLC. It was plenty big for our 5-man team.

Our computer guru, Milo, manned the phones, and mined the web for information regarding our clients, and their enemies. I'd given the team a couple of days off. No calls, no homework, nada. We would be up to our necks with Holly Santa Cruz, and planning for that job was to start on Wednesday, a full week prior to her arrival. The cashier's check from the client had arrived months ago, as promised.

We would be ready. However, I recognized a certain look which Milo showed when he knew more than he was telling.

Monday morning, I took a 2-mile walk, which I try to do 3 or 4 times a week. I can't get into jogging, with my hip replacement, but just walking the beachfront clears my head. It's also comforting that I have my compact Glock 26, 9mm, tucked in the waist band of my sweats, with my shirt pulled over it. I learned in Afghanistan, better to have it and not need it, than...well, you know the rest.

This morning was a beautiful day, highs in the 70s, a rolling tide, walking past "The Beauvoir", the final retirement home of Jefferson Davis, President of the Confederacy. The home had been magnificently restored to it's previous beauty after hurricane Katrina.

The storm washed out the entire first floor, destroying one-half the irreplaceable library. The government caretaker had been "too busy" to arrange for the safekeeping of the documents, but, you get what you pay for.

Highway 90, running right next to the beach, was filled with the usual workers, tourists, and travelers of most mornings, even though it was only 6 am.

With the massive I-10 interstate just a few miles to the north, it was much quicker for the people passing through from Mobile to New Orleans, or vice versa, to utilize that route. But, some of the retirees, or people not so caught up in speed, still took the more scenic drive on the old highway.

It runs from Jacksonville Florida to west Texas, and started in the early 1900s as "The Old Spanish Trail".

Those who care to partake of her scenery will not be disappointed with the parade of ante-bellum homes, and live oak trees, dripping with "Spanish Moss".

Josh was "kicking back" tonight, ordering pizza and watching a movie. He had arranged to take Jess and Connie out to dinner tomorrow at the famous restaurant, "Mary Mahoney's", on Rue Magnolia, in Old Biloxi. The menu and service were the best. President Reagan had dined on the lawn there when he was in office.

Josh figured he owed Jess, for swapping Hector's clothes at the hotel. And, he always went out of his way to make Connie feel like an equal sister. Indeed, Connie was a big part of the family. She was also one of the smartest, most instinctive people he knew.

Tuesday night came and the girls met Josh at his condo, as planned at 7 pm. He saw them pull up in one of the "visitors" parking spaces. The three of them hopped into the Range Rover and headed east on Highway 90, toward the restaurant.

In about 10 minutes they passed the "Beau Rivage", took a left on Reynoir for 2 blocks, a right on Water, and were right there in front of the famous dining establishment.

Josh had decided to wear a jacket tonight, since this was a strictly upscale place with linen tablecloths, real silverware, and great, but expensive, food.

They were seated immediately, and brought menus and the wine list. As is traditional in fine dining spots all over the south, the ladies menus had no prices.

Josh let his sisters peruse the selections for a while. Cooking, being Jess's vocation, had dissected each item, mentally, and nodded in approval.

"Can I have one of everything?" she asked. "I think your eyes are bigger than your stomach," Josh replied, "but get whatever you want."

Connie said "I went online for the menu, today, so I'm all set. I want the gumbo for appetizer and the stuffed snapper entrée." By this time Jess had decided on the two most complex dishes available. "I want the shrimp remoulade and the shrimp and crab au gratin."

Josh ordered for the girls, in true southern gentleman style, and added, "I'll have the gumbo as well, and the double lamb loin chops. Also a bottle of 'Belle Glos' Pinot Noir."

The sommelier delivered the Sonoma County wine and nodded his acceptance after drinking a small sample from the silver cup hung from his neck by a small chain.

Josh passed on his taste saying, "If it's good by you, it's good enough for me." The man decanted the wine to allow it to open up, and poured a small amount into the three glasses for a start.

The meal was wonderful, even Jess was impressed.

Josh finished the evening feast by ordering his one real weakness, southern pecan pie.

He drove the girls back to his condo. They had taken their time enjoying the meal for over two hours, so it was just past 9:30 when they arrived.

The girls headed home, and Josh thought how lucky he was to have two, very different, but equally wonderful, sisters.

Goldie Grows

I wasn't aware of my former self for quite a while. My previous life was lost to bone cancer. After a couple of months of special family attention, it worsened so that my physical body died. My being, or soul, as it is sometimes called, went to the "Land of the Spirits." It was then that I was given a choice by my "Spirit Guide", to go back to the "Land of the Living", or stay where I was, basically in heaven. A place where you never get hungry and you never died. I had asked the guide if I went back, could I return to the ones who I had loved on earth. My request was granted, and I "mysteriously" returned to the Flowers' family, as a puppy, all over again.

I had made the decision because I loved them, and I knew that they loved me. I had helped them through some difficult times, and wanted to be with them, even if they never needed my help again.

Within a few weeks of my "accidental" return, I began to recognize things from my past life with the Flowers'. The gentle bay breezes were one of the first. The voices of the family around me, and the way they insisted on calling me "Goldie", or "Goldie II." I instantly identified the aroma from the cigars smoked by the older one they called Grandma Doris. I even remembered Princess, the cat, and I think she recognized me.

Best of all, I recognized the shape and earthy smell of the garden, tended by my adopted Mom, Karen. This piece of land was cherished by her, and I started to recall the days I spent by her side while she planted, weeded, and watered. On hot days, I would sit under the nearby magnolia tree, but never to doze. I always kept other creatures out of her small patch of "farmland."

This, and the way they had of including me in the family, was why I had made the decision to return. I know I did the right thing.

This new life with the family was just as good as my first experience...in many ways, better. Josh, the young, 13 year-old boy who had picked me from the shelter, was a fine young man, today.

He had joined the U.S. Marines, just after 9/11. He was sent to a place called Afghanistan. He won medals and promotions, but one day he was wounded in action, basically ending his Marine career.

His two sisters, Jess and Connie were both in their early 20's, and were in the midst of beginning successful careers. They still lived at home, so we were able to see a great deal of each other. They were positive spirits, and fun to be with. My adopted Dad and Mom, Tom and Karen Flowers respected me, and treated me like their own "four-legged" daughter.

The traditional Sunday dinner usually included Karen's Mom, Grandma Doris, and Doris' boyfriend, Max, with whom she lived. Max wore clothes which were in strange colors, usually tropical combinations of orange, green, and lilac...all at the same time, with white patent shoes and belt as accessories. At least that's what I was told. I lived in a mostly "black and white" world, but with Max I think I can tell the colors sometimes.

Doris usually showed up stumbling and slurring her words, before eventually excusing herself to the back screened porch where she could smoke her sweet cheroot stogies.

Since Jess had graduated from culinary/hotel management school, she had become the top chef in the Flowers' kitchen, with Connie and Mom assisting.

After dinner, Doris usually passed out from too much wine. Dad and Josh (and I) would go into the family room and watch sports on TV. If we were lucky, it was football season and Dad was able to watch his favorite team, the "New Orleans Saints." I knew they'd win it all soon, I could just feel it.

Dad said that they had been "robbed" so many times in recent years that they were "due." I didn't doubt him.

Tom Flowers was one of the head administrators at the "Beau Rivage Hotel & Casino", on the "strip" in Biloxi. He had been a meteorologist with the rank of Major, in the Air Force, and was stationed at Keesler AFB in town. One day his unit was de-activated, it was a few years ago. His Air Force management skills had been just what the "Beau Rivage" was seeking when he applied there.

All of this added up to the reason I was so happy to be here. To be loved and respected by these wonderful people...this is where my loyalty lay. It was a good life.

The Star Arrives

Holly Santa Cruz arrived in her private plane on Wednesday, at 11 am. Her advance team for stage, sound, and effects had been in Biloxi since Monday. The reporters, photographers, and tabloids had been camped out for 4 hours.

I had arranged with a friend of mine who ran the airport, to bring her in through a non-public door, escorted by Kenyon and me through private areas, and had my Range Rover parked in an inconspicuous area. The plane had been instructed to pull to a certain point on the jet way, where reporters had no line of sight.

Thus, when Holly pranced down the stairs of the Lear Jet, we whisked her away, through the airport, to my SUV. The press was there, 100 yards away, trying to figure out... where was Holly? The entourage brought all the bags through the airport, flashbulbs going off in their faces, for nothing. A stretch limo I'd hired for the people, and a Ford Explorer we used for the bags, headed toward the hotel.

We entered through a back door at the hotel, and once again, swapped keys on the way up. Her suite was only slightly larger than my parents house, about 3,000 square feet, including kitchen and full bar, and we had two of them. No problem, the hotel was footing the bill as they do for all big entertainers, and there weren't many bigger than Holly.

We had adjoining suites this time, because there were only two, this size, in the hotel. Kenyon and I allowed Holly to acquaint herself with her "room", while we checked the baths, closets, under the beds, and installed the metal detector on the entry door.

The large entourage arrived about 30 minutes later. They had all been pre-registered as well, just in more standard sized rooms. There was a knock on our door. I glanced at Kenyon as he moved to a defensive position inside the room. "Who's there?" I asked, standing to the side of the door. "Julio," came back. "What's the word?" I asked. "Gringo" he repeated.

I opened the door. We used code words in case he was being coerced into trying to trick me. If he had answered "friendly," then I knew we had a problem. We had a problem, but it was only Clete. Julio said, "He was knocking on the door where me and Half Track were staying."

"He told us that he was a friend of Holly Santa Cruz. I figured anyone wearing this much jewelry, must belong to somebody, so I decided to take a chance," Julio said.

I let him in the room and the metal detector went off like a 3-alarm fire. "My jewelry, I guess, he said sheepishly." Holly came out to greet him. "Search him," I told Julio, while Kenyon and I watched. "Gun," yelled Julio.

Kenyon and I immediately raised ours. Julio expertly took the weapon away, "Smith & Wesson snub, 38 special," he said. I was not a happy camper. "Up against the wall," I yelled. "Take your boots off, slowly," I said. Sure enough, a little one shot derringer, was inside his right boot. "What else are you carrying, what else?" I demanded.

"Nothing," he replied with tears in his eyes. "OK," I said, "strip. All the jewelry, pants, jacket and shirt." He looked at Holly to save him. She didn't move a muscle. I walked him back through the detector again. This time he was without any weapons, and the alarm stayed silent. I noticed he was holding his breath that the alarm didn't go off by accident. That could have proven to be fatal, not by gunshot, but by heart attack.

"Sit on the chair," I ordered. I threw his clothes to Kenyon, "Check em out," I asked. About 10 seconds later, Kenyon yelled, "knife, a switch blade." I looked back and saw a horrified Holly.

"Julio," I said, "cuff him." "That's not necessary," Clete whined. "We'll talk after you're secured," I came back. Julio put the flex cuffs on in 5 seconds, flat. "Thanks, Julio, good job. You can go back and keep 'Track' out of trouble, we can handle this, now."

We sat down facing Clete, Holly to my left on the couch, in a pair of shorts and a t-shirt. I had pre-warned Holly in the Range Rover on the way to the hotel. Our tech guru, Milo, had traced a $200,000 deposit made just last week into Clete's account, back to a holding company owned by Holly's estranged husband, Billy Wade Monroe.

Also, Milo uncovered the fact that Clete had a police record for extortion and attempted kidnapping, which Holly knew nothing of. It was all starting to fit together.

"Where did the $200 thousand come from last week?" I demanded from Clete. "I,I,I don't know what you mean," Clete answered timidly. "I don't have any money." I threw the bank statement in front of him. "Is that your name, Cletus Moon?" I asked.

Clete broke down, "I wasn't trying to hurt you Holly, you've got to believe that. Billy Wade just wanted your schedule so he could tell you he was OK with the divorce...no more lawyers and courts. Said you wouldn't return his calls, so he had to tell you himself."

Holly was remarkably cool. "He could have had his lawyer call my lawyer, that's all it would take," she responded.

"How big a fool do you think I am? That's why you were bugging me about these guys, and their security plans," she said pointing at Kenyon and me.

"You didn't care about me, just the money he paid you for information."

"I told you all I knew, because I trusted you. Plus, you promised, no guns, why should I ever believe another word you say?" she stormed back to her room and slammed the door.

Five minutes later, hotel security and two Biloxi police officers took Cletus Moon into custody, illegal possession of a firearm, concealed weapons, etc. But our plans were severely compromised, yes, severely.

Now what? Holly's "soon to be ex" had rehearsal schedules, make up times, probably room numbers, and our names, too, everything Holly knew. What could I do?

I knocked on Holly's door. It took her awhile, but she answered, red eyes and all. "I'm sorry to be the one to do this," I said, "but we agreed, this job is about you, and no one else."

I followed-up, "We can't stay here. All your people know their job. You've done this act before, and you can probably do it in your sleep."

"I think we should move you, and let the crew continue their set-up jobs. We can bring you back for the shows, then disappear afterward," I said. "But move to where?" She asked. "I'm not exactly low profile, or unrecognizable. He'll spread money around and find me in a few hours, and he's not looking to have a talk."

She started crying again. As much as I wanted to I couldn't give her a hug, and say everything was going to be OK.

Holly added, "He's probably with a few of his fake cowboy buddies. You know, trucks with gun racks." I hoped she was right. Trucks with gun racks we could handle, but I worried that Billy was getting more sophisticated, weapons wise. I hoped I was wrong.

I started developing a plan. Not plan B,C, or even D...but a plan, nonetheless.

I asked Holly, "He's under a restraining order, right?" "Yes," she confirmed. "OK," I said, "you call your attorney, tell him to contact Billy's attorney, 'today', tell him to relay the message that it's going to get even more ugly, now that we're on to him."

I needed to figure out some possibilities, there were huge holes in our old strategy, but there had to be things we knew, that Billy Wade didn't.

I asked, "Holly, do you have a double? Someone who looks enough like you to do any of the risky moves in the videos?" "Yeah," she replied, "but she's in Nashville." "Good," I said, "you call your manager and get her here, today, and in secret. No one can know," I emphasized.

"You do that, while I make some calls. Things are starting to come together," I said as positively as I could. Her eyes brightened, she liked having a plan. I could tell. I went back into Holly's 2nd bedroom, and started making calls.

In about 45 minutes There was a knock on the door. "Housekeeping," said a woman's voice. I looked out the peephole and saw a uniformed woman with a cart.

"It's OK, I told Kenyon." He questioned my lack of caution, "You sure, Josh?" "Yeah I answered, I'm real sure." I opened the door and the woman walked in with a pillowcase. When she raised her head, Kenyon relaxed. It was my sister, Jess. Kenyon had met her before.

I brought Jess into Holly's suite. "Holly, meet Jess, Jess this is Holly". "I know," said Jess. I explained, "Jess is in management here at the hotel."

"She's also my sister, so you can trust her." I smiled kiddingly, "I'm well aware of her background, believe me. She's going to help get us get out of this jam." Holly walked over and gave her a hug. Jess didn't know what to do.

Jess pulled a hotel housekeeping uniform, black sneakers and maids hat, out of the pillowcase. Holly looked questionably at me. "These clothes are your disguise, I said. "When the time is right, you and Jess will push the room service cart to the employee elevator."

"When you get to the ground floor, make a 'U' turn, and I'll be outside the door, 20 feet away, in the Range Rover, I'll have some sweat pants and a top you can change into for the trip."

I continued. "Now, once we get settled, who are the two members of your travel group you can't do without? "My makeup pro and my hair stylist," she answered. "That's what I figured," I said, "and, if I can assume that, so can Billy Wade. The moment he thinks you're hiding, he'll latch on to them."

I continued, "When's the "double" coming in?" "I got lucky," she said. "She'll be here in 3 hours, but not on my plane, I rented another one for her."

"She'll be wearing a black wig, no one would connect her with me," she said. I was impressed. "Call her now," I said, "tell her a huge man will spot her on the entry ramp, with a sign for Ms. Dubay. Tell her to go with him."

"Now, call your makeup and hair people. Ask them to bring all their stuff, including their cell phones, up to this room, now, because you need a full preparation, just like for a show. Tell them you're going out for a night of fun. Anybody they tell, will be part of the diversion."

"Also, Holly, put the outfits you'll be wearing for the two shows into the pillowcase. Dresses, shoes, jewelry, everything." Holly looked at me, and held up four fingers. "OK, make that four pillow cases," I said, and she smiled. I went on, "And change into that housekeeper's uniform."

I had squared everything with Dad, during my earlier phone call. He didn't like using Jess as part of the ruse, but the last thing the hotel needed was bad publicity. He had to call his GM, Mr. Rutland, to get final approval, and he concurred.

Here's how it was going to work. Step one was to get Holly, and her hair and makeup people to a safe house, I had one set up. Next was to get her "double" into this suite, where she can eat and stay comfortable for three days, earning money for doing nothing but risking her life. Sounded more and more like Afghanistan to me.

After that, all we had to do was to sneak Holly back into the hotel the next two nights, and out after her performance, un-followed, back to the safe house, with no incidents...piece of cake, right!

Another knock came at the door in 10 minutes. It was the hair and makeup artists.

I let Holly look through the peephole, and she confirmed them. We let them in. "Cell phones," I said as I extended my hand. You never knew who they were going to call.

Holly nodded for them to comply. "You're going to be gone for a couple of days," Josh said. "It's gotten to be dangerous here, so we're moving Holly, and she wants you with her," he added.

"Mr. White, here, will transport you from this room to where Holly will be staying, in about 30 minutes. You are to tell no one," I stated firmly.

"I've instructed the switchboard to allow no calls in or out of these two rooms, for the 3 days. They've also disabled the internet connection on the computers."

The hairdresser, Siegfried, complained, " We're going to be confined and held out of communication, against our will? That's absurd, I'll have no part of it."

"Fine," Holly interrupted, "you can quit now, just leave," she said adamantly. "If you're not willing to help me, I don't need you." Siegfried, paled by her comment, knew where his paycheck came from. "OK," he said, "I'm with the program." The makeup artist, Yolanda, was nodding, really fast.

Josh explained, "You all know the trouble Billy Wade Monroe has been giving Holly. Word is that he's in town looking for a fight. None of you want that, do you?" Both of them shook their heads, in what looked like genuine fear. They must have witnessed some of the rocky marriage.

Josh continued, "We just found out Billy Wade paid Clete, to reveal Holly's schedule to him, so we have to change course, and change fast." Josh looked back at Holly, and told her the timetable.

"We're leaving in 10 minutes, please get changed and grab your show wardrobes. Do you mind if Jess helps you? Holly looked at the group assembled, she was scared, but tough. "Sure, Jess, come on back, you can be a big help."

There was another knock on the door. Josh motioned the hair and makeup duo to the couch, Kenyon took his defensive position in the room. Josh went to the door, looked through the peephole.

It was Julio. This time Josh didn't even have to ask. "Gringo," Julio said. Josh let him in and reviewed the plan. "Half–Track" was picking up and delivering the double to the room, here, sans cell phone. The double's name was Angie, he had learned.

Angie was to stay in the room for the duration, with "Track", who would be relieved every 12 hours by one of the other two men Josh had hired, either Drake or Pete. Two men guarding a decoy. It didn't make sense, unless you were the decoy.

During the performances, since everyone would know that Holly was onstage, the extra man would be pulled off the decoy, to help with stage security. Holly and Jess came out of the bedroom in costume. Josh was amazed not only at the change in appearance, but the similarities between Holly and Jess.

Yes, there was certainly no hiding Holly's physical attributes, natural or not, she was hot even in a potato sack, but size-wise, they were close.

Holly had the foresight to wash off most of her makeup. They each had 2 pillow cases. It looked like they were prepared. Josh looked at Julio, "Give me 10 minutes to get the Rover, I'll click the radio mike twice. Then you can send them down."

A few minutes later, right on cue, the two "house keepers" jumped in the back seat of the Range Rover, putting their pillow cases in the cargo area.

"I bought some light workout sweat pants and t-shirts in bags by your feet. The windows are blacked out so no one can see in. Get out of those uniforms, in case we run into anyone who saw you leaving. Put the uniforms in the bags. Jess can return them to the hotel when this is over."

We drove the two blocks west, and entered I-110 north, heading out over the Biloxi Back Bay. I wasn't worried about a tail, because Milo had scanned the vehicles for "bugs".

He'd be doing that every day, for the duration of the job. You couldn't be too careful. We were dealing with a man who had lots of money, a history of violence toward women, and a big ego.

Billy Wade Monroe could hire the best investigators in the world to find Holly. My bet was that he wouldn't do that because he wanted to keep that pleasure for himself.

We got off the Interstate link, and in a couple of minutes, pulled into an oyster shell driveway, right in front of the Flowers' family home.

Dad had called Mom on a land line and made sure she was OK with guests for two or three days. She was concerned, but trusted our judgment. She was waiting on the front porch when we pulled up at 5 pm.

Mom was smiling, as always, and wanted to welcome our temporary "guest", and make her feel at home.

Dad had agreed, as did his boss Mr. Rutland, his job at the hotel was all backroom, human resource management. No one could connect us to him.

Billy Wade would waste his time searching "high end" hotels within a 100 mile radius, and never think of this place.

He could find the apartment where I lived, and my office address. Once he found out Holly was missing, I was sure he'd "trash" both places. He wouldn't find anything there. I told Milo to go to the office, to get his expensive gear out, before we left the "Beau Rivage".

The Hideaway

I looked in the back at Jess. "Smile, Mom is worried." Holly asked, "This is your parents place?" "Absolutely," I said, "you'll be 100% safe here. Let's unload, Kenyon and the others are right behind." Jess and Holly got out and walked toward the house.

The front screened door opened, and Connie walked out on the porch, wondering what was going on. Then she locked eyes with Holly Santa Cruz. "Oh My God! It's not," she looked at me, "Tell me I'm dreaming."

"Inside," I said, "family meeting." We sat at the extended dining room table, because we knew Kenyon, his two passengers, and Dad, would be here shortly. "Mom, the garage done?" "All set, she said."

We used the garage just for storage, an extra refrigerator, etc. We could pull one car in if there was a hailstorm or something, but she had to make a much larger space for the Range Rover. I didn't want it seen from the road. "Be right back," I said. "Jess, make the introductions."

I came right back in after getting the SUV in the garage, and saw that Jess and Connie were falling all over themselves being warm and receptive to our new guest. Even Mom was taken aback at what was happening. "I just can't believe that in our little home, we have a 'Super Star' as a companion for a few days, I'm honored."

"OK," I said here's the deal..."No, me first," Holly cut me off . "In my business, you get tough, or you get eaten alive," she said. "I've been lucky," she continued, "Did I work hard to become successful, yes, do I have a little talent, yes again. But the are loads of talented people out there."

"But with that success, there is a price," she explained.

"Everyone wants to be around you for a reason. Money, fame, or in some cases, not mine, sex, drugs, whatever." She continued, "Now, this family, who I don't know, and who doesn't know me, risks their lives, takes me in when my life is in danger. To me, you are the Super Stars, and I'm grateful."

I was impressed. Mature beyond her years. I'm sure Colonel and Ms. Canfield had something to do with her perspective.

Goldie started barking, which meant Kenyon and Pete were here. Kenyon was driving a loaner van from a local Ford dealership, where I had a friend. The van would be untraceable.

He parked it at the far side of the house, anyway. I didn't want it to appear as if you were trying to hide it, just put it where it was not quite so obvious. Dad pulled up right behind. Jess let Goldie in and she was magnetically drawn to the new person in the group.

She slobbered on Holly, and I yelled, "Goldie, no, get down." Holly said, "It's OK, you have no idea how good that felt." The others came in and we began our meeting.

Dad sat at the head of the table at the spot we had saved for him. It was tradition. I introduced him to Holly, and he said, "I was able to speak to Colonel Canfield this afternoon. I told him you were in good hands."

"You can call him later on the home line," he added. With that, I said, "No cell phones." I put out my hand, and Connie, Jess, even Mom passed their phones to me. About 5 seconds later, Holly gave hers up too. Now we were all equal, in the communication world.

"As I was saying earlier, here's the plan, soup to nuts. Sleeping, I'll be on the couch, Kenyon and Pete in the kitchen on an old airbag I have. Siegfried and Yolanda, left bedroom, Holly, right bedroom..." "Josh", Connie interrupted, "I have a suggestion." "I'm open," I said, "this is a first for me too."

She asked, "Why don't you put Holly and her people upstairs, where Jess and I are? It's more private, and convenient for the show preparation, which is why they're here, and upstairs is safer for her. Jess and I can bunk downstairs."

Of course, I thought. This isn't the barracks at Parris Island, it's a place for Holly to be safe, and get prepared for her performance.

"Connie, I knew there was a reason I liked you, you're so darn smart." I looked at Holly, "OK by you?" I asked. "You're in charge", she said. "OK, Siegfried, Yolanda, why don't you go upstairs and get Holly's clothes hung, things in place, etc."

"I know the first show isn't until tomorrow night, but from what I understand, you two are critical to Holly's image. Just close the door so Goldie doesn't follow you and eat your make-up or something. We'll get her bed, and Jess and Connie's basics out in a few minutes."

Once they left, Josh thought he could talk about plans more openly. Goldie wouldn't eat make-up, but a closed door was a good thing.

We three are positioned as I said before. "Kenyon," I said, "Have Julio come in and meet Goldie." He got on the radio, and two minutes later, Julio was standing in the dining room, playing with Goldie. "She will be in the yard, if it's not raining, on the screened porch if it is "

Her hearing and smell are better than ours." Julio looked at me, sideways, "Alright, better than most of ours." Julio smiled, as he played with Goldie some more. "Julio will be outside the fence, somewhere. And now that Goldie knows his scent, she won't be barking at any false alarms."

Drake will be relieving "Track" on Holly's double, "What," said Jess, "you have a double?" "Usually just for the video stunts, her name is Angie," Holly said. "No she doesn't look like me close up, but on a video shot next to a smoking volcano, or underwater, it works, she's about your size, Jess." I started again, "Drake's partner Pete, will be relieving us during the day so we can stay fresh for "show time."

"During the day, we stay low profile. No phone calls, none." I looked at Mom, she nodded, she had removed the land line phone, and computer from the girl's room upstairs.

"Dad works as usual, Connie and Jess, no work for you."

"It's your job to stay with Holly during the day, can you handle it?" "We'll do great together," Holly smiled, "I haven't had real girl friends in ages." Jess and Connie were nodding their approval.

"Next phase, the show. This is where it's tricky. Everyone in the civilized world, knows where Holly Santa Cruz, will be, tomorrow night at 9 pm. On stage at the 'Beau Rivage'," I said, redundantly. Billy Wade's guys will be looking for her, and you can bet, they'll have lookouts to see from which direction she approaches."

I said, "That's why this location is perfect for us. We'll take Kenyon's loaner van and get on I-10 west toward New Orleans for a few miles. We'll drop down onto Highway 49 south, in Gulfport, right near the airport.

The hotel has a couple of large vans they use to shuttle the "quarter slots people" in from the airport, not the big limos they send for the high rollers, that's what they'll be looking for. At 7:30, Dad has permission from Mr. Rutland to commandeer one of those shuttle vans for an errand. We'll swap cars at the Wal-mart parking lot, at 7:45. We'll drop down to Highway 90 and we're 10 minutes from the casino."

"Anyone who sees us, will figure we are coming from the airport, with old folks in tow. If they are smart enough to make the connection, they'll think we're staying in New Orleans. Kenyon and I will come to the back of the casino and bring Holly, in through the private entrance to backstage. Dad will return to the casino right after us in the loaner van, and park it behind the rear entrance, taking the casino van back to the front of the hotel."

"After the show, about 11:30, I understand," Holly nodded. "We'll take the loaner van out highway 90 towards Mobile, then cut off at Highway 57, catch I-10, west, and be back here in 35 minutes, total." I asked, "Observations and/or problems?" "What about during the show?", Dad asked, "What's the stage set-up?"

"Well," I started, "I know the 'Beau Rivage' has doubled it's own crowd security team. I can't see anyone rushing the stage successfully. Plus, I don't think even Billy Wade is dumb enough to try anything in a place that public with casino cameras everywhere."

"We'll have Me, Kenyon, Pete, and Drake, positioned for any emergency. Half Track will be with the double, Angie, and then Julio stays here, with Siegfried and Yolanda."

"Oh no," said Holly, "I'll need them to help me during the

show, I can manage the makeup and hair, probably, but no way can I go through 2 wardrobe changes alone."

I answered, "I don't trust them with your life, do you? They could tell someone in your crew what's going on, even accidentally. People are notorious gossipers." I finished, "I don't have an answer."

"I've got a solution," Holly said, "but I'm afraid to impose even more," she said, looking at Jess and Connie. Holly went on, "It's not experts I need, it's just helpers, laying things out, putting thing away properly for the next show, someone I trust," she finished.

It was like all the air was sucked out of the room. All eyes on Tom Flowers, they were his daughters. Finally, Dad said, "They're both 21. I'm afraid for them, but I don't think Billy Wade or anyone else would see them as a threat, as long as he doesn't know who they are. It's up to them."

The girls started jumping and squealing, Goldie was excited, just because they were excited.

Holly said, "Thank you, friends. I'll have most of the day tomorrow to show you how we do things. You'll be great."

"Some conditions," I said, bringing the celebration to an end. "If we get into a situation, you two, just like Holly, will do exactly what I, or Kenyon tells you to do. No questions, no hesitation. Are we clear?"

A whole lot of enthusiastic yeses followed. "Secondly, my first priority is the safety of Holly Santa Cruz. All other considerations are in second place." More nods. "Lastly, you will remain backstage at all times during the show, and you will both be 'mute', not one word to anyone."

"If they ask about Yolanda or Siegfried, you shrug your shoulders. Holly, I need your help here, keep people away from them, and call them both Mary, or nothing, but not their real names. No one from the hotel will be backstage to recognize Jess, and they don't know Connie."

"I'll keep them away, don't worry, I won't let anything happen to Mary, or to Mary," she winked at the girls. "The crew is afraid of me. I'm their meal ticket," she added.

I looked around, the sun was setting, and Julio was already in the shadows, somewhere. That was his training.

"OK, meeting over", I said. "I think it's time to eat," I heard Dad say. Jess looked at Holly and asked, "Would roast chicken, with green beans be OK? I have enough for two meals, and the beans are from Mom's garden."

"I'm having what you're having," Holly answered. "And those two upstairs, will also." We added the additional "leaf" and filled the dining room table, with Holly, Jess, and Connie eating at the smaller kitchen table. Before I started eating, I took a large plate of food and a no-spill glass of tea, out to the dock.

I figured Julio would find me. He did, and I sat and talked while he ate. This guy was a lot smaller than Kenyon, but no less deadly.

He parachuted to the ground during the first "Gulf War", much like me, a 19-year old kid, scared to death at first. He helped introduce the U.S. Military to leaders of the Iraqi resistance. The resistance had an Arabic name for him which I can't pronounce, but it means "silent death."

I took the plate and headed back through the yard. Goldie was holding sentinel duty.

I went to the kitchen to get some food and tea and sat at the table with the three young women. Everyone was starved. It had been a long day. I finished at the same time as the girls. I guess I learned to eat fast in the Marines, and they liked to talk. It worked out.

Connie and Jess cleared the tables and were putting things in the dishwasher. Holly leaned over to me and said, "You don't know how much this means to me. For the first time in years, I can relax with people, enjoy their company, and not wonder what kind of game they're playing. I make lots of money, last year, over 50 million dollars, my accountant says, and I'd trade it all for a family like this."

"Thanks, I appreciate that," I said, then to inject some levity into the conversation, I followed with, "but you haven't met my Grandmother yet, and you won't either," I laughed. So did she.

She got up to help the girls in the kitchen. Mom said, "No, Holly, you sit down, they're fine." Holly answered, "Just because I'm me, doesn't mean I'm too good to help." Mom wouldn't give in. "Holly, this is my house, and you're our guest, and our guests don't clean, no matter who they are."

"You can help prepare, but cleaning is out." "No sense arguing with her," I said. "She's treating you the same as she does her own sister."

Accepting defeat, Holly said, "I can deal with that. I don't mind being treated like family," and sat back down.

The night was quiet, no problems. The next morning Jess and Connie made breakfast, I noticed that Holly was helping with breakfast preparation, a job which Mom had approved.

I figured she was probably clueless in the kitchen, but she was holding her own, even coming up with a couple of extra things to throw into the pan.

They were making one of my favorites, "crazy eggs", which is just scrambled eggs combined with whatever else we had in the fridge. Today they added bell pepper, turkey sausage, red onion, green peppers, and chopped tomatoes at the end.

Julio had appeared in the house, so everyone was enjoying the concoction, with toast and coffee. Holly laughed, "Two more days of eating here, and I'll be on 'Weight Watchers'," she said.

It was nice to see her laugh. Dad went off to work, the 3 girls went upstairs for their first "wardrobe session", and I checked in with the others back in town, on the land line."

Milo and "Track" reported "all clear." Milo said that our office hadn't been vandalized, yet. That was good news. We had a difficult time getting insurance the first time.

I had left Pete to observe people arriving at the hotel, and he reported seeing an unusual number of Texas license plates, not just at the "Beau Rivage", but at all the other casinos, starting with the largest, like "The Hard Rock", and working their way down to the "holes in the wall."

I guess the search was on, and Billy Wade Monroe was leaving no stone unturned.

I took the opportunity to call an acquaintance I had in New Orleans, named Clarence Boudreaux.

I had met Clarence at a law enforcement seminar in his city last year, and we hit it off pretty well. He was ex-Army, 82nd Airborne, as tough as they come.

He had been with the New Orleans Police now for over 10 years. Between Mardi Gras and Katrina, he had pretty much seen it all.

I asked him if there was much on the street about Holly and Billy Wade. He seemed surprised when I asked the question. "Man, we were just talking about that. There is some sort of search on at the hotels, restaurants, and other fancy places, for that gal."

"They started at The Ritz Carlton, and The Roosevelt, and they're working their way down the food chain. They've also staked out Antoine's, Commander's Palace, and Arnaud's. I heard that there's a $10,000 price for her whereabouts," he added.

"You know anything?" he asked. We weren't good friends on that level. "No," I said, "just wondering how wide they're casting the net." He laughed.

"She's supposed to be here in town," I volunteered, but everybody knew that, I wasn't telling him anything which wasn't public information, she'd been booked at the "Beau Rivage" for months, "but she's probably gone back to California," I concluded.

"But if I hear anything, I'll call you," I lied. We said our goodbyes, and hung up. It sounded like we had been lucky to find out the dirt on Cletus Moon. I wouldn't have wanted to be ambushed by Billy Wade Monroe. Milo had saved the day, so far.

I was more worried than ever, but was also happy that the search was focusing on the "high end" places.

The Delivery

The preparation of Holly Santa Cruz, for her show, began at 3 pm. In deference to her new "backstage helpers", she was wearing the most difficult outfit first. She got dressed with the girls watching Siegfried and Yolanda ply their trade.

I had snuck out with Mom, to go to the store. We were running out of food, and everything else. I came along wearing a New Orleans Saints cap pulled down, sunglasses, and a parka. When I got back, Holly was dressed, but with a tan raincoat over her, and Nike running shoes, both to protect the outfit.

At 7:15, I drove the loaner van toward our rendezvous. Kenyon and Pete followed in Connie's Jeep, but we switched the license plates with those of the Range Rover. I couldn't have someone see us and trace the car to Connie. We met up with Dad at the parking lot at 7:45 on the dot, and he took the loaner, while I took the van with the "Beau Rivage Logo".

Dad was going to wait 10 minutes before driving back to the casino, then park in back for our getaway, and reposition the casino shuttle van back in front of the hotel.

I had extra keys to the loaner, thanks to my friend at the dealership, so we wouldn't have to see each other in public. Then Dad would drive home in his own car. It went like clockwork. No one paid any attention to us as we pulled behind the casino.

But, there's always one thing, isn't there? The private stage door was locked and bolted. Some overzealous casino guard had probably secured it. I walked back to the van to think. Where did we go from here?

We had two choices, We could pick the lock, maybe, but what if it triggered an alarm? The other thing we could do is wait 10 minutes for Dad, but what if he didn't move the loaner van to the back right away? He knew we wouldn't need it until 11:30. The longer we sat out in the lot, exposed, the less I liked it. "Headlights"!

I flinched, but saw it was Kenyon and Pete, as they drove up in the space beside us. We talked through the windows, the girls listening intently. What to do?

Connie said quickly, "Josh, give me that Saints cap you're wearing, let me have it." "What's up.?" I asked. She outlined her idea. "I'm the only one here that no one knows. The staff spots Jess, and someone might get some ideas. And, Billy Wade probably knows what you and Kenyon look like,"

I nodded to that. "I'll hang out front, there are lots of other pretty girls out there, I'll pull the cap down low, I'll blend in with the crowd, until I see Dad." "Why the cap?" I asked.

"What's Dad's favorite team?" Connie grinned. "The Saints," I admitted. "He'll see the cap, he'll see me, and find a way to talk to me."

"Anyone have any other ideas?" Josh asked. I'm afraid for Connie, but she's right, no one knows her or what her role is in this operation. I'm sure Dad will see her, especially with the cap, and it's his daughter.

Connie said, "Josh it's a natural. There are always people outside the casinos, I'll pretty much go unnoticed, except to Dad."

Kenyon looked at me, "It could work." he said. I gave her the cap, it was much too big. She adjusted the band so it would still be loose, but not look like she had a basket on her head, gave us a big smile, and strolled confidently away to the front.

Six minutes later, Connie returned with a big "two thumbs up" sign. The door opened a minute later with Dad waving us in. It was 8:15, we were behind schedule. Not a good beginning, But it could have been worse.

Show Time

Holly was immediately in her element, and back in control. First she inspected the stage, while the girls unpacked her wardrobe, laying everything out as instructed earlier this afternoon. The stage was perfect, and all musicians accounted for. Holly was getting bombarded by questions, to which she kept saying firmly, "Later." She looked over to see Connie and Jess getting the same, but not so deferential, questions. "Stay away from them. Siegfried and Yolanda are fine, but they couldn't be here, so these two are filling in. I've got an opening in 38 minutes. Whoever isn't ready, don't come back tomorrow." I looked at Kenyon, we both smiled, but he said what I was thinking , "Man, she's tough."

The band began warming up outside, and we could hear the crowd growing. I knew that Pete and Drake were on either side of the room. Hotel crowd control was positioned, sitting with their backs to the stage. The stage was 4 feet high, no views would be blocked, and Holly wouldn't see them either. Kenyon and I watched our flanks, the right and left stage entrances.

The room started shaking... "Hollee, Hollee, Hollee," the crowd was chanting. Then there was a giant flash of smoke, getting our attention. It wasn't a bomb, and from that smoke, Holly Santa Cruz, appeared seemingly out of nowhere. She was wearing an all black body suit (it didn't have a zipper that I could see, it looked "spray painted on"), black patent stiletto heels and belt, and carried a black whip. Her first song was the number one single from her latest CD, and when the band switched to the melody, the crowd was in a frenzy.

"I've had some hot sweaty times with you", the song began, and the audience went wild. She sang in a husky voice, with a

smooth, sensual rhythm. Three songs later was her first wardrobe change, she disappeared, the band continuing with a solo by the drummer. We were backstage, on opposing ends, she reappeared into our vision in less than 2 minutes, she gave me a thumbs up in passing. I guess the girls did well.

Holly was greeted wildly again, as she picked up like she had never left. After one more set, and the last wardrobe change, we were done. The show ended at 11:30, right on schedule.

The crowd, inside, was still chanting for more, as we were making our getaway. Kenyon walked casually out the private door. He scanned the parking lot, the loaner van was there, and there were no threats in sight. He waved for us to follow.

We jumped into the loaner van, Kenyon and Pete into the Jeep, and we pulled out of the parking lot, taking a right on the strip (Highway 90), and headed east. Once we caught our breaths, Holly said, "The girls were great. They moved like pros." "You're the one that was great," Jess said, "We couldn't see, but we could hear, and the fans loved it."

"Well," Holly said, "this kid's exhausted." We had an easy, smooth trip home. No traffic at this time of day. We made it back in 30 minutes. Holly fell asleep on the way. Mom and Dad were still awake, of course.

We filled them in on a few details, told them the girls got an A+ from Holly, but I said the rest could wait until tomorrow. Holly went upstairs, and was greeted and pampered by Siegfried and Yolanda.

Jess brought a pitcher of iced tea upstairs, with 3 glasses. She knew about dehydration. Mom and Dad went to bed, and Julio had disappeared into the night. One night down, one night to go. Their luck had held out, so far.

I called Connie over. "How does she get that black bodysuit on? Was it paint?" Connie said, "Trade secret, I'll never tell," she smiled and walked away.

I knew I'd be seeing that, all night, in my dreams.

The critical show was the next evening. Billy Wade Monroe didn't like to look like a fool, and him not finding Holly sure made him look foolish. But I had a little diversion planned for him. Dad helped me pull it off, with a little help from his friend, DeWayne Holmes, the chief of police in Biloxi.

Dad had helped Dewayne's son get out of an embarrassing jam once. Nothing illegal, but it would have been used against DeWayne in the next election.

But that was tomorrow's plan of action. Tonight everyone needed some rest. Pete said he'd take the first shift of 3 hours. I would be on 3 am to 6, Kenyon 6 to 9.

The next morning I woke to muffled voices and aromatic smells. Jess and Connie were at the kitchen table with Kenyon. I staggered over to the coffee maker, grabbed a cup, and started planning. I offered Kenyon the couch, but he declined, having 6 straight hours of sleep last night.

Kenyon and I reviewed the plan. Billy Wade had been badgering reporters, hotel clerks, and cops, to find Holly, with no luck. More than one of DeWayne's men had gone to their chief, and asked about arresting Billy or one of his men, for attempted bribery. DeWayne declined. There were never any witnesses. A waste of time.

But now, we were going to use Billy's arrogance to our advantage. One of the policemen he had tried to bribe was going to help us. He would call Billy and verify that Holly would be arriving at the show tonight in a stretch limo from

New Orleans, with a police escort. The policeman said he found out, only because it was he, who would be the escort, from the Mississippi State Line on I-10, to the hotel. Hook, line and sinker, Billy swallowed the bait.

Billy told the police escort that when the limo got onto I-110 and passed over De'Iberville Road, he would see an 18 wheeler on the shoulder and a second one a quarter mile ahead. He should flash his lights at the second "big rig" and hit the gas. Lastly don't look back, it would be an accident.

The Last Night

A stretch limo was doing about 80 mph on I-10, behind a Biloxi Police cruiser. One thing about following police escorts, you rarely get a speeding ticket. They turned off onto the 4-mile stretch of I-110 which crossed Biloxi's Back Bay. About half way to the casino, the police car blinked his lights and accelerated his custom engine to about 120 in 10 seconds. No way the limo could keep up.

An eighteen wheeler pulled out of the right shoulder and blocked the road between the limo and the police escort. In the rear view mirror, the limo driver could see a second rig pull out and block them from behind.

They were trapped, water underneath them, and boxed in. Two cars from the left shoulder slowly approached the limo, one in front, one in back. Billy Wade Monroe got out of the lead car. He had a silver 45 caliber semi-automatic.

Billy couldn't see where Holly was in the car, because the windows were blacked out. He pointed the gun at the black driver wearing a small cap, and said, "Unlock the doors or I blow your head off." He heard the doors click open.

Billy Wade stood back and said, "Get your ass out here for a whippin you little bitch, you can't get away from me." The left side doors opened outward, and sitting there were 4 of Biloxi's finest, including Chief DeWayne Holmes, himself, in uniform and pointing their weapons at Billy. The black driver had lowered his window and trained his Glock on Billy's head.

He held up a badge, and yelled at Billy Wade, "You with the gun. On the ground now! Place your weapon on the street and your hands behind your head."

"Let's see," Chief Holmes said, stepping out of the limo, "illegal possession of a firearm, threatening a police officer, assault with intent to kill. Hmm, I'll let you calling me a 'bitch' pass, but this is for trying to bribe my men," and he kicked Billy in the ribs.

Holly and the girls were getting ready at 6 pm. Josh yelled upstairs, "Can I come up?" "Only if it's super important," Holly answered. Josh went up the stairs.

There was the group of Jess, Connie, Siegfried, Yolanda, and Holly. Holly had on some skimpy shorts, and a t-shirt, Yolanda applying makeup. Josh held out his cell phone.

"Just got the call. Billy Wade Monroe and 5 of his guys are in the Biloxi jail, and they won't be out for at least 3 days, according to the Chief. They're in deep trouble. The Chief called a press conference. Billy's done!"

The girls started screaming, Holly started sobbing, "I can't believe it," she cried, "My nightmare is over. I'm free." Josh answered, "It may not be over, but you've got a vacation." Holly went over and grabbed Josh around the neck...Yolanda screeched, "Holly, your make up, you've got a show to do." Josh looked at her, and said "Rain check?" Holly nodded thanking him with her eyes. "OK," Josh said, "but same precautions as last night.

This time we'll come in from the east, in our own cars, but it's still the same set-up for the show. He could still have some men left out there."

The show went off without a hitch. Josh even allowed himself to see the entire opening, *"I've had some hot sweaty times with you"*, she is fabulous, he thought to himself.

He snapped out of his trance, and walked further backstage to see the girls. All was in order, and again, at 11:30 pm they piled in the cars, but this time, went straight up I-110, and were home in 20 minutes. Kenyon and Pete followed about a half mile behind, on the lookout for a "tail." There was none.

At home, Dad pulled out 2 bottles of Champagne, and glasses of all types. "Compliments of the 'Beau Rivage'," he said.

"Last night was the largest volume night we've ever had, and tonight looked even bigger."

Everyone had a toast to Holly, and she toasted back to us. "I'm beat," Holly said, "but I'll be right back." Five minutes later Holly returned is some jeans, an old blue shirt, and sneakers. She looked at me and said, "Josh, let's take a walk."

Out by the dock, she asked me. "I want you to be my permanent security team. You can travel with me, your men too. You'll make double what you earn here. I feel safe with you...even closer, if you know what I mean. Think about it, talk to your team."

"I've already hired someone for Vegas this weekend. You don't have to decide tonight." Josh closed his eyes for a few seconds, imagining how it would be. Him and her together, all the time, but he knew the answer.

"Holly, I don't have to think about it. I can't do it, and I'll tell you why. First, I have a 'home field advantage' here which I would lose in any other city. Knowing the Chief, the casinos, and the local roads are a huge plus for me." Josh continued, "Out in some other city, as far as protection goes, we'd just be a few more guys with guns, nothing more. At least professionally. That's why we get so much of the business that comes through here. Ask your Dad. He'll tell you the same thing. Why do we have so much trouble finding Osama Bin Laden? He and his cohorts know the territory, we don't."

"Secondly, I don't want to be one of those hangers-on you spoke about to us. How long would it take before you started looking at me as just another person, dependent on you? That would kill me."

"Thirdly, and most importantly, I care about you. I care about you, a lot. That's a bad mixture." Tears welled in Josh's and Holly's eyes as she hugged Josh for what seemed to be a long time. But it was too short for Josh.

Holly stepped back and said, "I'm not used to being told no, I always get what I want, except this time."

"And I respect you for your honesty. I care about you too, more than anyone I've known." Instead of dragging out the letdown, she turned and walked back to the house. About 30 seconds later Josh followed, but he sensed movement to his right.

Julio said, "I didn't hear, wouldn't have been right. But I'll bet that was tough." "You'll never know," said Josh, "You'll never know."

The next week, two large envelopes came in the mail, addressed to Connie and Jess. Dad had an inkling, so he waited until they were together.

"Oh, girls, these arrived today postmarked from L.A. for you." They tore into them. The contents were identical. First was a check made out to the addressee for $50,000. It was drawn on HSC productions, and read "for services rendered."

The smaller envelope was an invitation to the production of Holly Santa Cruz's newest music video. A hand-written note said, "Keep May 14-18 open. I'll send my plane for you, more later." It was signed by Holly.

The girls were stunned. They looked at each other and hugged each other in a special moment.

The Neighbors

Josh was looking forward to some serious "down time" after the hectic and exciting 3 days with Holly. The girls had told him about their "bonus" from the singer, and he knew it was really appreciated. They had stuck their necks out for a stranger and deserved it.

Josh had gone to the grocery and discount department stores, early that morning. You know, he thought while he was pulling into the parking lot of the local (big chain) grocery store, you never knew what you were out of, until you got home. This was especially true fro Josh. He would be away from home, on a job with a client for 4,5, even 6 days at a time. Then once he walked into his condo he would discover that there was no food, the milk had gone bad, no coffee, nada. At this point in time Josh would usually resign himself to ordering out for pizza, and walking up to "Stacey's", a little breakfast place down overlooking the gulf.

Well, not this time, he told himself. He was a grown-up now, owner of a company. He was a taxpayer with responsibilities for others. But this time, he was going to take case of Josh, he promised himself.

After visiting the discount store, Josh drove the ½ mile to the market and immediately splurged at the seafood department, buying 12 jumbo shrimp (still an oxymoron), at foolishly overblown prices. He couldn't help but smile at the absurdity of it.

Josh bought a pre-made (but very good) gumbo base, which allowed him to skip the preparation of the "roux" and eat dinner while he was still young.

He added a six-pack of Corona, some rice, a loaf of French bread, butter, and a small container of frozen yoghurt for dessert.

Then, he purchased coffee and toast for the morning, and even some boneless chicken breasts, pasta, and a bottle of decent red wine for later in the week. Adulthood had reared its' ugly head.

Josh got back in the Range Rover and pulled out of the parking lot heading toward his nearby condo. The wind whistled through the Rover, as it had many times before. Yes, Josh thought, different cars, different times, different dog. Well, maybe not, to more than one of those responses. Josh hooked a quick left and in under a minute drove up in front of the Flowers' home. He jumped out, leaving the car running. Josh burst through the front door and yelled at his Mom, Karen, who happened to be the first person he saw on his way through the house to the back yard, "Takin' Goldie with me, OK?"

"No problem," Karen yelled, "you staying for supp..." he was already gone. "Goldie, ride?" Josh shouted, and an 85 pound, yellow ball of love was on top of him in an instant. They wrestled, and then ran toward the front gate, Goldie jumping "shotgun" in the Range Rover, the window already half way down.

He was just got home to his own parking lot when he noticed his neighbor's, the Levy's, door slightly ajar. This was odd, he thought. These were quiet people who kept to themselves. It was very unlike them to be so careless as to leave the front door open. Goldie had followed Josh upstairs, but had sat against the wall and stayed, when he motioned her to do so.

He listened at the door and heard some rustling noises, inside, like someone was searching for something. Josh rounded the corner, let Goldie into his condo, put the 2 grocery bags down quietly, and closed his condo door behind himself.

Josh examined the lock on the front door. It had been forced open.

Well, he could call the police, and hope they got here, but that wasn't his way. He looked over the railing of his 3rd floor condo and saw the Levy's car was missing.

Things just got more interesting. He peeked in the door and saw the back of a man going through some drawers in the kitchen.

Josh pulled his Glock 19 out of the holster under his windbreaker and stepped into the condo. "Hands on your head," Josh ordered. The man froze. Of course, Josh couldn't see what he might have in his hands. A gun, a knife, could be anything.

"Hands on your head, last chance and turn around," Josh commanded. The man finally obeyed, and Josh came face to face with a bearded old man, probably in his 80's.

"Who are you and what are you doing here," Josh demanded.
"None of your business," the old man spit back at him.

"Really," Josh said, "I'm making it my business. The Levy's are friends of mine.

"I'm not talking," said the geezer. "OK, I'm calling the police," Josh said. "Breaking and entering, attempted burglary, I'm sure they'll be amused." "I'm sitting on the couch," the man said, "my back hurts," and he went to the living room couch and sat down.

Josh was stumped. What to do? His best bet was to wait until the Levy's returned, but that could be in 5 minutes, or several days.

They were always going on cruises, sometimes for two or three weeks at a time. Josh decided to press the issue. "Show me some ID, or I'm calling the police," Josh threatened the man. The man thought about it for a minute, and reached for his back pocket.

"Slowly," Josh warned. The old man pulled out a wallet, which looked older than Josh, and handed it to him. He opened it and pulled out a Florida drivers license. "Benjamin Levy?" Josh asked.

"Yes, brother to Sol, brother-in-law to Belle," and the man folded his arms. "But, why did you break in?" Josh asked. "None of your bees-wax," said the geezer, "This is between Sol and me."

About that time Josh heard someone at the door, "Hello," came a familiar voice. Sol Levy entered the room, with Belle right behind him. "Bennie?" Sol questioned. "I thought you were in Boca."

"I came to get what is mine," said Benjamin. "Oy vey, the broach," Sol replied. "Yes, our mother's broach," said Ben.

Josh interrupted, "Mr. Levy, if this is your brother, I'm out of here. I just saw someone going through drawers searching for something, and I thought you were being robbed." "Bennie," Sol asked, "you were searching our home?"

"Yes" the man said, "she was my mother too, I want the broach. It meant more to me."

"I'm leaving," said Josh, "this is obviously a family matter." But, Josh added, "Sol, your brother doesn't scare easily, so call me if you need me."

Sol replied, "No son, my brother, Bennie, he survived Auschwitz. What would scare him today?"

I took two steps back. I had no idea what horrors he had witnessed, but, he could be as rude to me as he wanted, no complaints.

I left, and went next door to my condo. The Levys would work it out.

There sat Goldie, licking a melting pile of frozen yoghurt off my floor. I sat down with her in the middle of everything and asked," Pizza OK, girl?"

"Whoof, whoof," she gave a resounding, yes!

The Prince

Prince Dunhr al-Said was on a shopping spree. He was the eldest son of a King who ruled a small, but extremely wealthy middle eastern country. His tastes ran the gamut from race horses to mansions, yachts to Lamborghinis. His highness was staying on his 285-foot yacht, appropriately named "Royalty" in protected international waters off the coast.

The Prince was considering a buy of a group of casino/hotels in the U.S. He certainly included the properties of "MGM Resorts International" in the list he had developed. MGM's properties were premium and besides the "Beau Rivage", encompassed the MGM Grand, Bellagio, New York - New York, and many others.

One of the other groups being considered by the Prince, was the "Hard Rock Hotel and Casino", with hotel locations in Chicago, Tampa, Los Angeles, and more, with casino/hotels in Las Vegas, and Biloxi. The Biloxi location was almost next door to the "Beau Rivage". The Prince decided that this would be a much "lower profile" way to compare these two, without having to battle his way through crowds in "Vegas." And, both hotels were new, thanks to "Katrina."

"Special Corps" had been recommended to handle landside security for the Prince by an independent defense contractor in the middle east. It was run by one of Josh's former commanders in the Marines. He had been contacted by the "business manager" of the Prince, and was offered $50,000 for a half-day job.

After hearing the scope of the job, Josh agreed, and the money was wired into his business account the next day. The Prince was well protected at sea. A dozen special forces bodyguards, all well armed, four, 50 caliber Gatling guns, a non-military version of the Boeing AH-64 Apache helicopter with helipad, and some people had said, twin torpedo tubes fore and aft. A veritable destroyer. All this was worthless on the ground. His guards had no weapon permits, most couldn't speak English, and they didn't know the layout of the area. That was Josh's strength.

The basics of the plan were to meet the Prince and 4 others at a private airstrip just off I-10, called "Lundy's Heliport".

Josh was familiar with the place, as it was mainly utilized by entertainers and "high rollers", shuttling in from New Orleans.

From there they would take two limos to the hotels, which were only 20 minutes away from the heliport. The Prince had a 90 minute tour scheduled with the general managers of each hotel. His list was very specific as to what he wanted to see. Executive offices, security central, luxury suites and penthouses, retail shops, and the private gambling rooms for the "whales" as big spenders were called. Then back to the Heliport, and the safety of the "Royalty". All in all, 5 hours, tops.

At exactly 10 am Josh heard the thumping of the approaching Apache. He and Kenyon turned to look, as it headed directly for them. Josh hadn't seen one of these in almost 3 years, and had never seen one which didn't have all the usual military firepower on board. I wonder if they have all that equipment back on the yacht, Josh thought. Of course they do, he answered himself.

Two men in expensive looking Italian suits came over to Josh. "My name is Imud Salaam, the business manager for his Highness. This gentleman is Yusef Wadi, manager of security." We shook hands with them both, introducing Kenyon and me. Imud continued, "I have verified that the tours are on schedule, is everything secure on your end?"

"Yes," I said "hotel security is fully alerted, but not as to the nature of the visit.

There are two armed Biloxi police officers in each limo, all four are men, as you insisted. One will drive, the other will be in the front passenger seat. We have two motorcycle officers in front and in back. My associate, Kenyon White, will ride in one car, I, the other."

I added, "The Mississippi Highway Patrol has a car every two miles along the route, your call to the Governor was taken seriously".

I also have two "undercover" men on the floor of the casinos, themselves. We have private parking and entrances at both hotels."

"Allah be praised," said Salaam. "It would appear that we are in good hands." He added, "As we discussed, his Highness will choose which of the cars he will be in." "And," he added, "do not speak to his Majesty, unless he asks you a question." I assured him that the protocol had been reviewed by everyone who might come in contact with the Prince.

Salaam turned and nodded toward the helicopter. A young man, no older than I, exited the chopper door and walked to the second of the two cars, the door being held open by a bowing Imud Salaam.

The Prince was wearing a sports jacket, khaki pants and Sperry Topsiders. He was accompanied by another large man in a suit...looked like a 58 extra long. He entered the second car along with the business manager and security chief, the big man got into the first car, and the rear suspension strained.

Kenyon and I had already decided that he would be in the first car, I in the second. We took a last look around, and saw that they were leaving 2 men behind to guard the Apache. I was sure there were weapons on board.

Once the motorcade began, Salaam looked at me and said "This is his Majesty's attempt at low profile, dressing... "Silence," said the young man swiftly. "Who are you to explain my actions?" "A thousand pardons, Highness," Salaam was groveling.

The Prince looked at me and asked, "What do you think of my western attire." Uh-Oh, I thought...careful.

"It is not my job to critique your wardrobe," I said. "It is my job to protect you from those who would harm you." The Prince smiled, "You see Salaam. He knows his job. You should stick to yours."

"Yes, Highness, a lesson learned," the man said obsequiously.

The tours were set, beginning at "The Hard Rock", 777 Beach Boulevard. We pulled behind the hotel. I had called the G.M. when we were 5 minutes out. They were ready for us. We parked close to the door. Kenyon and I were out immediately, in flanking positions on either side of the two cars.

The large man emerged from Kenyon's car, and the 3 passengers from my limo walked toward the hotel's General Manager, Mr. Lamb, framed by the doorway. The G.M. walked right past the Prince and shook Salaam's hand, "Your Majesty, it's an honor that you grace our presence."

Salaam turned the G.M. toward the young man, and said, "You are mistaken, sir. This is his Majesty." I thought Lamb was going to have a stroke. His face was beet red, and he started sweating profusely.

"I apologize your Highness. How stupid of me." "I should buy this place just to fire you," the Prince replied tersely.

"My face is on the internet in a thousand places, maybe a million, and you couldn't do your homework. You're a fool." What a start, I thought. Two police officers accompanied us inside, leaving the other two, to guard the limos. We began the tour in the security center. It looked like a NASA command center, video monitors everywhere. Everything was new.

The hotel had just opened 2 months ago in June. It was originally supposed to debut September of 2005, 23 months ago, but hurricane Katrina washed that away...literally. While the Prince was in the secure room, we had little to fear. I made an excuse and took a quick trip to the men's room. I got into a stall, closed the door, and called Jess on her cell phone.

She picked up on the first ring. "You at the hotel?" I asked. She was. "Get Rutland (the G.M. of the "Beau Rivage") on 'Google' right now. Find out whatever you can about the Prince." I explained what had happened at the "Hard Rock", and she understood.

I got back to the security room, the Prince was asking questions. No one had missed me.

We toured the executive offices and penthouse suites. Now the hard part. The penthouse elevator stopped on the main casino floor.

Even at this time of day, there were hundreds of people there. Most of them pulling the slots like zombies. We went to the "high stakes" rooms where, primarily men, played "hold-em", baccarat, and mixed poker games. Some oriental players gave the Prince the "eye", like, who are you?

The large man walked over to stand beside him and the men quickly went back to studying their cards.

"I've seen enough," the Prince announced. Great, I thought. I dreaded walking through the casino to the retail shops. Salaam started to say something, then wisely thought better of it.

We departed the same door we had entered, the cops and Kenyon both calling ahead. This time the Prince picked Kenyon's car, and we were off to the next block, 875 Beach Boulevard.

We pulled in the back, and Mr. Rutland was beaming. Once we got out of the cars, he walked straight over to the Prince, gave a slight bow, and said, "A great honor to meet your Majesty. It gives me a chance to congratulate you on winning the Polo championship of Dubai."

The Prince gave him a sly smile, but did not extend his hand to be shaken. He hadn't performed that tradition since we had been here. We went through the same routine as before. Once we got to the casino floor, I spotted Half Track. That was his one drawback, he was tough to hide. Of course, I saw an 80ish silver haired lady at the slots, who could have been Julio.

As we walked through the casino floor to the shops, everyone stopped what they were doing. Two cops, 3 men of Arabic origin, one of them a giant, Mr. Rutland, his assistant, Kenyon and me. Nine of us surrounding a young man in khakis, who was obviously in charge.

A drunk staggered out of one of the many bars, looked at us and said, "Who's the kid?" He was lucky that Kenyon got to him before the middle eastern "Grizzly Adams."

Kenyon handed him off to one of the uniforms, who, turned him over to hotel security. He hadn't done anything wrong, just asked an ill-timed question.

At one of the stores, "The Fallen Oak Pro Shop" the Prince stopped and looked into the window. This was a shop for a nearby Tom Fazio designed golf course. The Prince was "taken" by the logo of an oak leaf dipping into the water. He turned to Salaam, "I'll take it," he said. "Your Majesty, which color?" He looked back. "Do I have to explain everything to you?" He looked at me.

"What do I mean?" he asked. I looked at Rutland. "Close the store. He wants everything in it." I looked back, the Prince was smiling.

"Of course," Rutland said. The store is closed. He looked at the store manager. She didn't understand. "You've made a big sale," he explained. "Go home. We'll ship tomorrow."

The Prince looked at me again. "I'm ready to leave." We left. Back at the heliport, they loaded back into the Apache and flew off into the Gulf skies. We were spent.

The next day Rutland called me and thanked me profusely for giving him a "heads up" regarding the Prince, after the faux pas at the "Hard Rock".

"I don't play favorites," I said, despite the fact that my Dad and sister both worked for him. "I just wanted to avoid a possible beheading." Rutland said, "I see what you mean...no I saw what you mean." We both had a good laugh out of that.

Weekend with Doris

After a long couple of days planning and executing the tour of Prince al-Said, Josh was looking forward to a quiet weekend. However, his cell phone buzzed during his Friday night of TV movies. It was Dad. "Hope you didn't forget about tomorrow, son."

"No, Dad, you mean Sunday, I'm all set for dinner." "So, you did forget," Tom Flowers said. "The show at the Senior Center which your Grandma Doris is in." Josh slapped his forehead. "Yeah, now I remember. Is there any way out?" he asked.

"Not unless you come down with bubonic plague, and then Doris will want a letter from the morgue," said his Dad. "OK, what time," Josh conceded. "Be here at 10 tomorrow," his Dad said. "The girls want to ride with you. They see you as their best chance of an early escape."

The seniors were presenting "Arsenic and Old Lace," by Joseph Kesselring from 1941. Grandma Doris was trying to make up for her disastrous attempt at "South Pacific" a couple of years ago, when she accidentally burned all the props, caused a car explosion, and damaged the Flowers' home.

Doris played one of the two starring sisters, her devious rival, Betty Malbon was the other, and Max played Mortimer's brother, Teddy, who believes he is actually Teddy Roosevelt. Sammy Pantolino played the leading role of Mortimer.

The play started off with mediocre performances, and went downhill from there. Grandma seemed to know her lines, but the timing was off. Sometimes she seemed surprised it was her line, and forgot her cues.

Early in act 2, Doris seemed desperate. Max came out on the stage, Doris looked at him and said, "Romeo, Romeo, where art thou fore sweet Romeo?"

Someone had the sense to drop the curtain. A spokesman came to the stage and said that Doris had taken ill, and would be replaced by a stand-in. Most people who knew Doris, assumed she was probably coming down with "red wine poisoning." In the middle of the second act, Doris stood in the wings and tried to grab the stand-in and take her place, but was stopped by two of the supporting cast. "They're stealing my lines," she said, "they're my lines," she repeated.

The family debated whether to remain for the duration, or evacuate the premises. It was decided that Tom and Karen would stay, Josh and the girls would go to home and await the return of everyone, for a Saturday afternoon gathering.

Josh pulled into the oyster shell driveway, and Goldie started a ruckus in the back yard. She wanted to be with Josh and the girls. Jess let her inside, and Goldie immediately ran to Josh. He started wrestling with her, and they both had a good time. He didn't see as much of her as he would like. He knew she felt the same way too.

In a couple of hours the clan arrived. Max and Doris stayed just long enough for Doris to apologize, saying she should go home and not expose the rest of the family to the flu. They gracefully let her use that excuse, then she and Max drove off.

Josh said playfully, " Well you got me here, now you've got to feed me." He, his Dad, Goldie, and Princess, went into the family room to watch college football. He stayed long enough to watch the first half of USC vs, Nebraska, which USC finally won 49-31.

Tomorrow was the traditional Sunday dinner. Karen called her mother that morning to see how she was feeling. Doris confirmed that she and Max be at dinner. "I wouldn't want to disappoint everyone, just because I'm not 100%."

"Anyway, I think it was food poisoning, not the flu. Betty Malbon made sandwiches for the cast and crew. I ate one of them, which was a terrible mistake."

"You know," Doris said, "Betty is a horrible cook. We'll be there at noon," she finished. Right, thought Karen.

The Shrimper

It was 6:45, Monday morning, and I was coming back from my walk on the beach when my cell phone starting beeping. The ringtone was Mozart, piano concerto #21...Milo! What was he doing up this early.

He usually worked on his sophisticated computer network until the wee hours of the morning. I answered with "Don't you ever sleep?"

"Not much last night," he answered. "We have a possible new client. I was in the office at 2 am, minding my own business, when someone came knocking on the door. He was going to stay all night and wait for you, but I told him to come back this morning at 9." "Who is he, and what does he want?" I asked.

"His name is Tran Van Minh," said Milo, "He's a shrimp fisherman, he wouldn't tell me any more than that. Said he trusted only you. Will you meet him?"

I thought about it. What can it hurt? We had a few days before our next scheduled job. "Yeah, call Kenyon and tell him to meet me at the office at 8:45. And one catch, you have to be there too." Milo complained, "Oh, that is so unfair, so not cool." Anyway, Milo agreed, and promised he'd be there if in spirit, only.

I pulled up to the office at 8:30. There were two small oriental men squatting on the curb, outside my office. There was a beat up, red pick up truck, which they had obviously used to get here.

I parked the Rover, and walked toward the door. I noticed that one of the men looked about 60, the other could be his son, or grandson, as the old man had the weathered face of someone who was used to spending a great deal of his working life in an outdoors environment.

They both rose, and performed a ceremonial bow. "Are you Mr. Frowers?" the older man asked. "Flowers, Josh Flowers," I answered as I extended my hand to take his." "Mr. Frowers, I am Tran Van Minh, this is my son Tuan."

We shook hands and I suggested, "Just call me Josh," I don't think I could have kept a straight face hearing "Mr. Frowers", during the meeting.

I saw Kenyon pulling up beside me. He got out as I was opening the office door. I waited for him at the entry. The men looked to him and I said, "This is my associate, Kenyon White. You can call him Mr. White," not knowing what he would do with the name "Kenyon."

I locked the office door behind, and the 4 of us went into our small, 12 x 12 conference room. "So why are you here, what do you need from us?" Tran began, "We here because Mr. Chief Holmes tell us you might be help to us."

"You mean Chief of Police DeWayne Holmes?" I asked. "Yes, Chief Holmes," Tran answered. "He no can help us, but say come see you. I offer to pay him, he say no."

Kenyon asked the '$64,000 question', "What's this about?" Tran looked nervous. "He not say Mr. White, he only say Mr. Frowers." There it was again, like nails on a chalkboard.

"Chief Holmes knows I work with Mr. White. Anything you say to me, you can say to any of us who work here." Tran looked relieved. I'm sure he had been worried about offending Kenyon. "My daughter is gone," he said. "She go away Friday, not come home. We want her back."

His son, Tuan, was considerably more fluent in English, and much more direct than his father. "Her name is Kim, which means 'golden' in our language. She's run away before, that's why the police can't help us. We think we know where she is, and who she's with," said the young man.

Now it was coming together, I thought. Tuan told us more. "She's only 17. She goes off with these older guys, does drugs, and who knows what else." If we can get her back, Dad can get her into the drug rehab clinic in Hattiesburg. She'll be 18 next year, and she won't go voluntarily. Dad wants to help her to clean up her life, get her a second chance." "The problem is," he continued, "these guys she's with are mean, crazy, always stoned, and have guns." A great combo I thought. One look at Kenyon, told me he agreed.

I spoke to them both, very slowly so that the older man could follow what I was saying. "I'm going to have to discuss this with Mr. White," I said. "We can give you an answer later today." Looking for an easy way out, I added, "Since Chief Holmes referred you here, I can give you a discount on our fee."

But it's still going to be $15,000 per day or partial day." They didn't blink. Tran, the father, gave me his business card. It said "TVM Shrimp Co., Tran Van Minh, owner." The background of the card was a drawing of four shrimp boats, with Vietnamese lettering on them. Tuan added, "That's an old card, we have six boats, now. We have one more to go." I looked at Tuan, questioningly. "Seven," he said. "Seven is father's lucky number."

Lucky seven, and my family is in he casino business, Josh grinned.

They got up to leave just as Milo walked in. "I'll give you an answer in the next couple of hours," I said. They walked out of the office got into the old pick up, and sat. They would wait, until I gave them an answer.

Kenyon, Milo and I discussed it. We didn't have anything else going this week, why not? We just had to be careful. These domestic situations were never as clear cut as they seem.

We agreed. I walked out to the truck. Tuan was behind the wheel. I went to the passenger side, and held out my hand to Tran. "We will help you," I said, "Starting this afternoon."

The old man was nodding his head and pumping my hand. He said, Thank you very much Mr. Frowers." "Remember, it's Josh, OK?", I answered. They drove away. I think I saw a glint of a tear on Tran's wrinkled face.

That afternoon, Kenyon and I drove down to an area called the "Point". This is the center of the fishing, shrimping, and oyster industries in Biloxi. This area is as far east as you can go, and still be on the Biloxi side of Back Bay.

We passed St. Michael Catholic Church, commonly know as "the fisherman's church," and only a little further up 5th St. was a 3-story, concrete block building with a sign reading "TVM Shrimp Co."

"Looks like we're here." Kenyon said. That's why I like him. He has a wonderful way of stating the obvious.

They were apparently looking out for us. Tuan met us at the front door, and directed us to the stairs. "The office is on the third floor," he stated. "The first two floors are actually a huge covered dock area, where the boats can pull in and unload their catch. Then we process on both floors surrounding the dock. It's very efficient. My father worked the past 35 years here."

"After Katrina, we had some damage, lost one boat completely. But father bought out two of his competitors who just couldn't make it." Tuan halted midway up the stairs, "He paid them a fair price, though. They were grateful."

I had no doubt. We finally reached the third floor. Tuan escorted us into his father's office. It was simple, but neat.

The best part was the large window where you could see all the way from the Highway 90 bridge, which linked Biloxi to Ocean Springs, to most of Back Bay, where Josh's parents lived.

Mr. Minh motioned for us to sit down. I had brought him our standard contract for services. And placed it before him to review. He never even looked at it, just signed.

"I pay you for two days work in advance." he said. In the corner of the room was a safe about six feet tall and four feet wide. It had to weigh at least a ton. He looked at me and smiled, "I know what you thinking" he stamped his foot in front of the safe, "Reinforced with I-Beam," he said. "No frall through."

He opened the safe, and took out three large stacks of bills. "Thirty thousand dollars," he said, "in advance. I looked at Kenyon. "We usually take cashier's checks," I said. "That's a lot of money for us to be hauling around today, especially while working."

Tran looked puzzled. "You take check from me today? I get cashiers check tomorrow?" I looked at Kenyon. He nodded.

For the first time in my short career I said "Mr. Minh, your company check will be fine." I called Milo to come get the check, and as I found out later that day it cleared the bank with no problem.

The four of us sat down at a conference table. Tuan spoke to his father in his native tongue for a couple of sentences, then looked at us and took over the conversation. "My father said I could speak for both of us and you would understand better. I am the oldest child, so it is customary."

"My sister," Tuan began, "I believe is with a doper by the name of Nguyen Chi Dung. He makes and sells drugs, mostly methamphetamine, but he deals some coke and heroin on the side. We got my sister back from him last year when she OD'd on heroin."

He added, "Nguyen dumped her in the parking lot of the hospital emergency room, and drove off. A nurse at the hospital knew father, and called him."

"Nguyen owns a trailer park just off Pass Road. The are about 12 units, mostly occupied by his people, all in different names. I don't know where he makes the meth, but he deals it at the trailer park."

"We don't know which unit my sister is in, or we'd try to grab her ourselves," Tuan concluded.

"No, you're doing the right thing," Kenyon said. "Nguyen doesn't know us, and our team are all professionals. Does your sister have a car?" He hoped, but that would have been too easy. "No," said Tuan, "she can't drive."

"I need to speak to your father," I told Tuan. He looked at me with suspicion. "No, we're good," I said, "I just need his permission for something." I looked into the worried eyes of Mr. Minh. To come this far through hard work and sacrifice, then have something as precious as a daughter taken from you by drugs, and gangsters, was killing him.

"Mr. Minh, we're going to locate your daughter and get her back." He smiled at me. "But, I may need your help. I have people who can listen in on cell phones, track emails, run computer checks on bank accounts. They are very good."

"So, you want what?" He asked. "I need Tuan," I said. "None of my people speak or read Vietnamese. I could hire an interpreter, but how could I trust them?"

I continued, "Tuan would not be in danger, he would work with my computer expert in my office, with the man you already met, named Milo."

Tuan interrupted, "I will do anything for my sister." "I still must have your father's permission," I said. Mr. Minh nodded, and we were halfway home. "Good, Tuan, be at my office at 6 pm. We should be set up by then."

I elaborated on my plan. "What we are thinking, Mr. Minh, is that we accomplish two things. One, get Kim back home so you can get her medical treatment, and two put Nguyen out of business, get him arrested if possible, so he's out of your life for good."

Father and son spoke rapidly, nodding and smiling. I needed no translation, they loved the plan. Now, if we could just pull it off.

I called Milo on his cell phone, to give him a head start on the phone numbers, email addresses, and bank accounts.

Then I got through to Julio, who would begin a recon mission on the trailers this afternoon.

Kenyon and I got up to leave, and Mr. Minh offered us a bag of shrimp from a small freezer in the office. We started to decline, but Tuan said under his breath, "You must take the shrimp, it seals the agreement. It would embarrass him if you did not." We both smiled and accepted the shrimp. "I'll see you at 6," I said to Tuan.

On the way, I called Chief DeWayne Holmes, thanked him for the referral, and broadly outlined our plan, stressing the point of putting a large meth dealer behind bars. He loved that, and I knew he'd help if we needed him.

By the time we got back to the office, Milo had 3 cell phone numbers, an email address, and two bank accounts, all registered to Nguyen Chi Dung of Magnolia Mobile Home Park, unit #3, just off Pass Road, not even 10 minutes from our office.

"Verizon only has one good cell tower close to him, so we can monitor that one and get 99% of his calls," Milo boasted. I told him about his new interpreter, Tuan, as I knew Milo loved getting "real time" information.

Tuan got to the office at 5:50, and sat with Milo, who had set up another listening post and computer monitor just for Tuan. Milo started streaming the past week's emails to Tuan, who was reading them at hyper speed. In about an hour, Tuan looked up, "They're expecting something big to happen, soon," he said, as he continued to read.

The phone calls began at 9:45. chatter was heavy. Milo was getting lots of good details. Hope was growing.

"Wait," Milo cried out, "he's calling someone." The call was picked up and all eyes went to Tuan, wearing the headphones. "They keep talking about 'OS', and 'OS Road," said Tuan, "Happening Wednesday night." Milo was taping the whole thing, as well. We all looked at each other blankly.

Just then, Julio called in. "I'm at the DQ, across Pass Road," he mentioned. "The girl's in #3. I saw her look outside when a dog was barking."

Julio said, "She looks like 3 miles of bad road, she's really strung out," he concluded. "I got close enough to hear them talking, but it's all gook talk," said my politically incorrect associate.

"Come on in for a while, then you can go back out," I said. "Got it," he said. In 10 minutes Julio strolled into the office wearing a cowboy hat and boots. I introduced him to Tuan, and outlined the story. "Does OS mean anything to you, or OS Road?" I asked. "I'll think about it," was his response.

Half Track was right behind him. He had rented a dark blue van, in case we had to do a "snatch and grab." "Track took up the whole reception area." At 6'6", 325 pounds, people didn't like messing with him.

His size alone, demanded respect, and I knew he was a former Golden Gloves champion, heavyweight, of course.

"Track," I asked, "does OS or OS Road mean anything to you?" "Sure, Ocean Springs, and Ocean Springs Road. Used to date a chick over there."

We all felt dumb, but got over it. It was a beginning. I believed we'd fill in some of the blanks in the next few hours.

Julio had tied a bandana around his head, changed his shirt, and laced up some Nikes. He would look different now, when he went back out.

All we could really do is wait for more information to cross the airwaves. If we knew when they would be gone, the "snatch and grab" would probably work fine, but that was only half the plan. We wanted to put Nguyen out of business.

More and more calls and emails were being intercepted by Milo and translated by Tuan. Then when Nguyen spoke to the buyers, it was in English. It appeared the buyer of the meth was a group of rednecks from near Pascagoula, about 30 miles east.

The meet was set for about a mile south of exit 57 off I-10, on Ocean Springs Road. We still needed a time, and the names of the buyers. I called Chief Holmes, he said he'd alert the DEA, Ocean Springs Police, and the State Highway Patrol. They could be "busted" at the buy.

Around 11:30 Tuan took his head set off, and stared ahead. "What," I asked. "Kim's part of the deal," Tuan said. "She's in on it?" I asked. He looked up with tears in his eyes, "No, they're selling her as part of the exchange." Needless to say, now we had to rethink our entire plan.

We all started thinking about possibilities. Finally Kenyon looked around the room and said, "The problem is, we don't know enough to have any chance of success." "Right," Milo said "But we still have at least 36 hours till the buy. Look at how much we've uncovered in only 6. I think we put a 'full court press' on intel, and see what we can develop."

"Let's get going," I said. "Track, you're going to Pascagoula, tomorrow morning."

"Nose around the biker places, see who's into selling 'crank'. Go home and get a few hours sleep first."

I thought about the situation and said, "Julio, you go back over to the trailer park for the next couple of hours. Then sleep, but have a position set up by 9 am where you can observe all the trailers. I doubt we're dealing with early risers."

"Milo, you and Tuan, once the chatter goes quiet, which I suspect will be soon, each of you grab a couch and get some sleep. "

"Focus," I said. "Tomorrow is critical, and it mainly depends on you two. We must find out the time of the buy, the exact place for the swap, and the location of the meth lab, and we've got to find out in the next 24 hours."

Tuan called his father and told him he would be away for a couple of days. After he hung up, Kenyon asked, "A little late to be calling, huh?" Tuan answered, "Father won't sleep much until we get Kim back."

Kenyon and I agreed to meet back at the office at 7 am. We would chase down whatever leads the team uncovered. I called Chief Holmes' office and left him a message to please call me when he got in. The night was restless, but I learned in Afghanistan the value of being rested and fed.

Dewayne Holmes called me at 8:15 the next morning. We needed the phone records for the past 30 days for Nguyen.

He was doubtful he could get them, but once I told him that it involved "human trafficking", he said he could get a court order in an hour. He would fax us the records. This was something that no judge dared deny us a warrant for.

At 11 am "Track" called in saying he was making some progress. He found some "speed heads" who took a liking to him.

You have to see the beauty in it. Who in their right mind would use him for undercover work? His size made him so conspicuous, he was inconspicuous.

Julio called and said that Kim was still in #3. Nguyen stayed in #5, all the time. Some new arrivals came in that morning, all heavily armed, and carrying speed with them. He said that 3 more, possibly 4, trailers were housing armed gang members. Great! I thought it was going to be easy.

At 1:00, the sweet sound of the fax machine started churning out pages of telephone numbers. I told Milo to focus on the most local exchanges first. The meth lab had to be close. Nguyen wasn't dumb enough to keep all the stuff with him, but he wasn't going to let it be too far away, either.

In 30 minutes we got 2 possible locations, an old warehouse in Gulfport, and a used car dealership on Pass Road. We focused on the warehouse. It belonged to Xuan Hoa LLC. "This means spring flower," said Tuan. Kenyon and I jumped into the Range Rover, set the GPS, and were in Gulfport in 15 minutes.

The warehouse was off the beaten path, and sat among a few other similar, poorly constructed buildings in a light industrial park. Women were coming and going. Most of them wearing aprons, some even had blue surgical masks over their mouth and nose.

We didn't see any guards or lookouts, and after 15 minutes, we got out of the car and decided on the direct approach.

Kenyon let his Mossberg hang down by his leg I had a Glock 19, and my right hand, in my pocket, the Glock 26 was in an ankle holster. We went around to the back door, it was locked.

I gave Kenyon the 3,2,1, signal, and he kicked in the door. A woman looked up at us and started screaming and yelling, in what I assumed was Vietnamese. Then more of them saw us and they all started a commotion, putting their hands up and ducking behind tables. We quickly did a threat assessment.

There was none. We looked around the inside and saw row after row of 6 foot tall aluminum carriers on wheels. Every one filled with loaves of bread. In the center of the room, women had stopped kneading the dough. Baking ovens covered the exterior walls. Then near the entrance was a container of baked and packaged bread.

It had large Vietnamese symbols on the cover, and underneath in English it read "Spring Flower Bread". "Made Fresh Daily." I asked for the man in charge. A slight oriental man came over, not making eye contact. He was afraid.

I asked if he knew Tran Van Minh. His eyes grew brighter as he nodded his head. I told him we had made a mistake. That we were sorry, but we were looking for Mr. Minh's daughter, and thought she was here.

"She not here," he said. I apologized again. I asked if he knew Nguyen Chi Dung. "Yes, he call my daughter every day, as he pointed to a pretty, young girl, but she no want to be with him. He druggie."

"Can I speak to her?" He beckoned her over to us.

I explained the situation about Mr. Minh's daughter, and asked her to please not say anything about our presence here because Kim's life was at stake. She nodded and said, "I don't talk to him, my Father tells him not to call again, but he gets wasted and calls anyway." I gave the old man in charge $200 in cash to repair the door, and left.

OK, we avoided a big mess. We got back in the Rover and I called Milo. "Give me the address of the car dealership, I asked." He did, and volunteered, "Owned by SEM, LLC, which means nothing," he said, "but SEM is part of NCD inc.", another link in the chain leading back to Dung.

"Southeastern Motors" had 8-10 clunkers in front. By their looks, they'd been there a while. We got out and pretended to be interested in one of the cars. A young, Vietnamese (I suspected) boy with wrap-around shades walked over smoking a cigarette. "That one is sold, cowboy," he smirked. "Really," I said, "How about that one over there?" I pointed a couple of cars over. "Yep, that one too," he said. I looked at Kenyon...BINGO, we thought.

Not to be obvious or memorable, I said, "Looks like it's not our lucky day," and we got back in the SUV and drove away. The office was only 10 minutes from here, so we went back and borrowed Milo's car to continue our recon mission. We drove back down Pass Road, and pulled into a Burger King across from the lot. We took a window seat sipping diet Colas.

There was a huge building in the back of the lot. It read "Southeastern Motors, Repair and Body Shop". We were home, no doubt. To verify, we drove down a small "service road" directly behind the large "Body Shop" building. Kenyon hopped out as I slowed. I went around the block, and he jumped back in on my return.

"Guy with an AK-47 sitting in a chair right inside the door," he said. "Couldn't see much more, they have the windows painted black." We both knew he'd seen plenty. We got back to the office and I called Chief Holmes. After an hour he called me back. This is how it was going down:

The DEA was getting a warrant for the body shop/meth lab, from a friendly judge based on an anonymous tip. They were going in at 7 pm., 3 hours from now. One down!

Also at 7, Swat and State Police would bust in on Nguyen in all the trailers except #3. Our team would snatch Kim at 6:55. We needed a family member to ID Kim, and my guys could get her out of the situation without her becoming entangled in the bust.

Very unorthodox, but I had brought them the case, and DeWayne argued for me to be included.

Nguyen was already a 2-time felon. Caught with guns and drugs in his living quarters, would keep him in Parchman for 20 years, minimum. Two down!

The buyers would get to the site, turn around and go home. They would be under surveillance and ID'd, which could prove useful in the future, but they walked on this one.

Sometimes, you take what you can get. Milo called Half Track and told him we had a 5 pm meeting at the office, I called Julio, he stayed on recon, I gave him the details. At 6:45, Julio, Kenyon, Half Track and I were in position. Tuan had parked his pick up, a block down Pass Road and was walking down the entrance of the Trailer Park.

At exactly 6:55, he knocked on the door of unit #3, and

spoke in Vietnamese. A man came and opened the door. He was obviously stoned, but carried a sawed off shotgun.

He looked at Tuan and without an interpreter, I was sure he told him to go away, and stay away.

Tuan stepped to the side, Half Track came around the opened door, grabbed the man by his belt and his throat, and hurled him, upside down, into the side of the next door trailer...lights out. Kenyon slipped in and caught another man reaching for a gun. Kenyon hit him full force with his fist into the man's Adam's Apple, and the man went down gasping for breath. I brought Tuan in with me and he pointed out his sister, passed out on the couch.

I grabbed her, and we ran outside, Julio had the rented van coming from the rear of the park, right toward us. Kenyon slid open the side and we all piled in. "Floor it," I said just as the door latched closed. He did, we were out on Pass Road in 10 seconds. I looked at my watch...6:58.

We rounded up the various cars and met back at the office. Tuan called his father, who was obviously overjoyed. Tuan wanted to take her home, himself, but I explained that our contract was not over until we delivered Kim to her father.

He understood that. Kenyon and I brought Kim back in the Range Rover. I wanted Tuan to ride with us. If his sister woke up, she might "freak out" not knowing us. Tuan would be able to explain the situation to his sister. Milo followed us in Tuan's truck.

We drove up in front of the shrimp company. There must have been 20, of what I assumed to be family members, outside, all yelling and jumping as we pulled to a stop. Kim was just coming around.

Tuan was telling her what was going on. I don't know how much she understood. She was very groggy.

Two men carried her inside. Mr. Minh grabbed Kenyon and me and hugged us while crying and speaking in Vietnamese. I guess he realized his language usage, and said "Thank you...whole family thank you."

"Wait," he said, "you both take bag of shrimp." I smiled, "Of course."

Doris and Max

The Flowers family was doing very well, in a middle class way. They were hard working people who had never been given anything, and were also proud of that. Connie's real estate career was starting to gain Momentum. She was the #3 agent in an office of 8. Everyone knew she'd be at the top, soon.

Jess had turned 21 earlier in the year so she was now consumed with learning the casino side of her management training at the "Beau Rivage".

Josh's business had been good, and his reputation for excellence was getting around. Josh had arrived at the house early this Sunday to share some extra time with Goldie, down at the dock. Tom Flowers had been promoted, again, and was now the assistant G.M., right behind Mr. Rutland, who rumor had it, was due to retire in less than 2 years.

Karen stilled filled in when needed at the library to cover vacations and such, but was primarily involved with community charities, her garden, and keeping her Mom, Doris out of trouble.

Today was another Sunday dinner at the Flowers' family. It was full of love, jokes, and telling tales of the previous week. Grandma Doris arrived full of wine, as usual.

Doris walked in with her boyfriend, Max, exactly at noon. Walked, is a very kind exaggeration of her gait that day, "stumbled" is more accurate. She swayed down her usual path toward the screened back porch. There she would light her chcroot cigar, watch the wind blow through the live oaks, and have another glass of wine.

Max was festooned in white and yellow polyester pants, pink Izod knock-off shirt, the usual white patent shoes and belt, and a straw "Panama" hat with a red feather in the headband.

He was a sight to behold. Max followed Dories obediently, opening the door for her and pouring her wine. They sat at the wrought-iron table and Doris rested her chin(s) on her chest, falling asleep almost immediately.

The rest of the family went about their business setting the table, placing chairs, etc. With Jess now mostly in charge of this weekly get-together, the menu had become decidedly more eclectic. They still used as much from the garden as possible, and Jess usually worked around a different theme for each dinner.

Today was "Asian" day. Jess had prepared spring rolls with dipping sauce plus a side of wasabi mustard, Chinese chicken with hoisin sauce, and Peking duck for the main course.

This was served with hot tea, followed with a very dry pinot gris wine. "Watch out for the wasabi, it's a killer," Jess warned. Sliced fruit from the garden was dessert, along with vanilla ice cream.

Goldie was looking forward to the duck, rinsed of all of the marinades. It was one of her favorites, and she could taste it, already.

Grandma and Max stumbled in to the table. The family sat for dinner at 12:30. The appetizer was excellent. Doris was eating her spring rolls, when she said, "These green mashed potatoes look great," putting a forkful of wasabi in her mouth.

Her eyes went red, her face sweated, and she let out a yowl which would wake the dead. "Awwwwwwwwwww, help me, water, water, ice water."

Connie went into EMS mode, and got a pitcher of iced tea from the refrigerator. Doris started "chugging" the tea, getting a lot of it on her, and on the floor. Jess brought a glass of crushed ice to the table and Doris kept shoveling it into her mouth, as she was screaming, "Hotttttt", over and over. Princess ran out from under the table after getting drenched with iced tea.

The family saw Doris reach sobriety in less than sixty seconds. This was a new record. After a few minutes, she had recovered.

"What was that?" she asked. "Wasabi mustard," Jess explained. "It tends to spice things up." Doris answered, "I know what you mean, honey, it almost did me in. Can I have some bread?"

"I'll get you some, Karen said, we've got some leftover rolls in the pantry." After the bread, Doris was back to normal...or at least normal for Doris. "Need some more wine," she said, and indeed, the world was spinning on it's correct axis again.

Tom and Josh retired to watch the Saints in the family room, Connie got packed for her "Open House."

Doris and Max went back to the porch. Max was consoling the woman, "Anyone could have made that mistake," he said. "Who knew what that wasabi stuff was, anyway?" Max tried to soothe her. He was smart enough to know that whenever her drinking caused a scene, Doris would revert to her role of the innocent victim. Max had been on to her tricks for years.

"Yeah," Doris said accusingly, "you'd think my own family would tell me beforehand that it was like swallowing a volcano. They just never think about me, I'm just like extra baggage to them, they don't pay attention."

Doris was posturing for her "Rodney Dangerfield...I get no respect" award, and feeling sorry for herself at the same time. This was a big part of her act to get attention from the family.

"You know," Doris continued, "I raised my daughters to be respectful, and what did it get me? Nothing, that's what, and now they try to poison me," she concluded.

"Well," started Max, "you're the one who got Jess started on this culinary career of hers. Taking her to that "Tex-Mex" place in San Antonio, and complaining about the 'bland food' everyone ate when you moved here." Max continued, "And beside the accident," he offered, "today's food wasn't bad."

"Yeah," said Doris, "I know that I deserve the credit for Jess finding a career, but they'll never admit it. They still should have warned me about the food." Max agreed with her, she was always right. "I'll be your taste tester in the future," he volunteered. "That way there will be no surprises at the dinner table, like today."

He added, "Or Doris, you could just ask what something is, if you don't recognize it." She countered, "And look stupid or senile...I don't think so. If I start slipping they'll have me in a home faster than you can say Grandma."

Max corrected her, "Now that we live together, they couldn't do that. We could get married if we had to. And I don't think you're giving them enough credit. Your family adores you, especially your grandkids, they really do. We just have a little misunderstanding every now and again," he concluded.

After another 30 minutes the older couple made their departure, no doubt to the Senior Center with tales of inedible food. Doris would be looking for sympathy. The couple left, weaving their way out to Max's rusted old Lincoln Towne Car.

Next stop, would entail a slanted retelling of today's events, to their friends. Doris would play the role of the victim she enjoyed so much.

Kenyon

Kenyon White was my first hire, and #2 man. He was an ex-Navy SEAL, a big part of our company, and a great person. He never asked for a favor. Never complained, never wanted special treatment. I had promised him a partnership in the company, for only "sweat equity" after he completed 3 years of employment.

That's why it surprised me when he called me at home early on Saturday morning. "I've got some personal situations back home that I need to get involved in," he said.

"Kenyon, come on over to the condo, lets talk," I replied. He knew that I would give him all the time off he needed. I just wanted to get comfortable with his request. An hour later he rang the bell and walked in.

We sat on the couch in my simple condo, and had some nice Colombian blend coffee. "What's up?" I asked. "It's my nephew, man, he needs some help."

Home for Kenyon was Virginia Beach, Virginia. Most of the SEALs either came though San Diego or Virginia Beach. I know what you're thinking, tough duty in paradise on either coast. It's not that way. SEAL training is one of the toughest tests of physical and mental endurance that one could survive.

Try running 8 miles in the sand, sometimes, if you think you're tough. Anyway, Kenyon needed my help. He wouldn't ask for assistance, just time off. "What can I do?" I asked. "Nothing, I can't handle," he replied. "Well, you've got me involved, like it or not."

"The gangs are getting bad up there," he said. "They're pressuring my nephew to get involved with them. Christ, he's an 'A' student, but that's not cool with them, they want more "bangers."

Sunday we flew via U.S. Air, through Charlotte, to the Norfolk /Virginia Beach airport. Virginia Beach was the largest city, in an area which was collectively called "Hampton Roads" (formerly called "Tidewater"). The "Beach" was a city of about 450,000 people, which along with four smaller cities comprised the Southside of "Hampton Roads" and was the center of a growing community of about 1.2 million residents.

The largest employers in the area were the Norfolk Naval Base, the largest naval base in the world, and Oceana Naval Air Station in Virginia Beach, home of the attack aircraft who flew from the 4 aircraft carrier groups based in Norfolk.

The city limits of Virginia Beach contained almost 50% water, hence the name "Tidewater." There were small inlets and marshes everywhere, plus the Ocean and the Chesapeake Bay. Kenyon's parents lived in a planned community built in the 70's and 80's called "Fox Run". Fact is, there weren't any foxes, and you only had to run from the frequent gunfire. The gangs had taken over. The worst of them was named the "Life Takers".

After landing, Kenyon and I rented a Jeep Cherokee at the airport and made a stop at a gun shop, on the way to meet the family.

Sunday afternoon I met Kenyon's parents after his father's sermon at New Bethel Baptist church in southern Virginia Beach. They were trying to raise money for expansion, so the service was a little longer than usual. The members of the church were not a wealthy group, but they were having bake sales, car washes, anything to raise the money. Reverend White had relied on God, and parental involvement to raise his children.

It had worked well with Kenyon and his 3 siblings. However, this next generation was different. Today's world was about drugs, whores, bling, and, "What can I get for myself, 'now'?"

We met Kenyon's uncle Matthew, on the church steps. He was genuinely grateful for our presence. He tried to give us his take on the situation, but he didn't understand the "gang culture", and the peer pressure that went along with it. He did understand, however, that he needed help.

That was a good start. After getting the few facts he knew, I decided that we also needed help. Tomorrow, Julio and "Track" would arrive, ready for action. Kenyon didn't like it, but I was the boss.

Kenyon's nephew, Dante, was a "straight arrow" kid. Despite being accepted by 3 universities for academic and social accomplishments, he was being hounded by the gangs to join them. The gang had also made threats against Dante's sister, Bonita, who was only 15 years old.

The gang needed someone like Dante, who had a clean record to "front" for their illicit drug acts. Such is life in the gang world today.

Kenyon and I took Dante and his girlfriend to a local, upscale, Italian restaurant called "Aldos." We all ordered and ate before talking about business. My veal chop, butter flied and stuffed with spinach and parmesan cheese, was the best I'd ever had. Once the main course was done, we started talking about the "situation."

Dante asked Kenyon, "Is this OK to talk about this here?" What he meant was with a "white boy", but I took no offense, I was the unknown factor at the table.

Kenyon answered, "I trust this guy with my life. Is that enough?" I guess it was, because Dante started talking. "They see me as a way to get into the college campus, with credibility. If an 'A' student is one of them, the kids will think it must be alright," he said. "This one leader, Tyrell, keeps threatening my sister, Bonita. He says she'll have it bad if I don't do what he wants." It's all him, the others don't care. I think he's got it out for Bonita."

"Where does this Tyrell live," I asked. "Down in 'Shadow Lawn', south end of the beach," Dante answered. "That's all I need," I replied. "Stay cool for a couple of days, the cavalry is on the way." He looked at Kenyon, who just nodded his head.

We were strangers here, no Chief Holmes to depend on, if we got into trouble. And, we were going to shake things up a bit.

But this was "family." Milo uncovered the "HQ" of the "Life Takers". It was a duplex condo down on 16th street.

They had been renting there for about a year, plying their trade of extortion, intimidation, and selling drugs. They had about 60 people in their network, all reporting to, and paying a premium to Tyrell.

Milo also hacked into their bank accounts and emails. Technology is a beautiful thing.

We decided to use the afternoon to become more familiar with the area around Tyrell's home base. We drove east on I-264 until the road turned into 22nd Street, about 8 blocks from the oceanfront. We went a few more blocks and took a right on Baltic for 6 blocks to 16th Street.

Tyrell's place was obvious. It was a one-story yellow duplex with lookouts sitting on the steps in front. The left side of the duplex was boarded up, fewer entrances that way.

There was a Black Lincoln Navigator parked in front, so Tyrell was probably home. I called Milo and gave him the plates to run, just to be sure. Milo called back with a confirmation that, indeed, the SUV was registered to a Timothy Tyrell Johnson.

Now for a little harassment of our own. I called the news line of WAVY TV channel 10, and gave an anonymous "tip" that a huge drug bust was going down in 30 minutes at Tyrell's address. I hung up and waited. In about 25 minutes a large white van with "WAVY TV 10" on the side pulled up in front of 520 16th Street, and a "News Chopper 10" helicopter was circling the home.

Kenyon and I started laughing. You could almost hear the toilets flushing from our place on the street. A young black man walked out to the front porch glancing from the news van to the helicopter. He was close to 6 feet tall, shirtless, and wearing a blue "do-rag" on his shaved head. He looked over at us, and strutted across the street to our car.

"What you two dog's doin' here?" he asked. "Just watching the show," I answered. "So far it's been fun. Heard the water pressure is down because of all the flushing going on." "How 'bout I flush your skinny white cracker ass?" he smarted off. Uh-OH, Kenyon got out of the car and walked over to stand by my window.

This wasn't in the plan. Tyrell pulled a knife out of his back pocket. "Why don't you start with me?" Kenyon responded. "I do most of his light work," he said, nodding toward me. "You Tyrell?" Kenyon asked. "What's it to you?" Tyrell came back. Kenyon said, "Well the description fits. Ugly, skinny, walks and talks like a bitch, yeah, I figured it was you."

Tyrell swiped at Kenyon with the knife, who quickly stepped aside, grabbed the man's arm with both hands and snapped it down, hard over his knee. The sound of his bones cracking, hurt me.

Tyrell almost went white, and in about 2 seconds the shock wore off so that he felt the pain. At least one of the forearm bones was broken, maybe both. Kenyon smiled and said "Now go back inside with the other girls so you can have a good cry." Tyrell started screaming and running toward the duplex. A couple of his boys started moving toward the car with silver semi-automatics tucked in their waistbands.

"Think about it, boys," I said as I raised the barrel of the Mossberg 12 gauge up to the bottom of the Jeep window. "Just tell your boss he should find a new place to work in. Far from here." Their eyes got big, and they backed off in the direction of the house. Kenyon got back into the car and we started to drive away when a reporter, a young Hispanic girl, walked over toward us. She got about 10 feet from the car, and said to both of us, "I saw the whole thing. He attacked you with a knife, and you defended yourself. My name is Maria Moreno, if you ever need a witness." "Thanks," I said, "but I doubt he'll be going to the cops."

"No, they usually come to him," she replied. "I'm in this area almost every week because of that thug." I thanked her and we drove off.

Half Track and Julio arrived the next morning. We met and decided on a plan of action.

Milo had discovered the weekly drug route and schedule through a combination of phone, bank, and credit card records. Best of all was the photo system at the toll booths along the way.

No one put a lot of money into protecting that type of equipment from hackers. For Milo, it was a snap. The route appeared come from the south, probably Miami or Atlanta, through Virginia Beach, up Highway 13, which ran through the less populated areas of Virginia, Maryland, and Delaware, then onto larger interstate highways to Philadelphia, Newark, and New York. It was a weekly run, one week south to north, the next week would be reversed, north to south. Tyrell was obviously a stop-over, swapping money for drugs.

Our plan was to eliminate Tyrell...well, really to have some other good citizen do it. It was two weeks past Labor Day so the streets and shops weren't as crowded as usual. Perfect for our needs.

Julio was staked out to watch the house. He would keep us in touch with the activity, and also snoop around looking for the cash the gang had stashed there. "It's either in the attic, or the crawl space," Julio surmised. "Tyrell wouldn't let the money be too far from him, and tonight is the swap." Julio was like a cat in the night, he'd find it.

We knew we couldn't find the meeting place by tomorrow, so we went with a remote controlled plan. Part 1, was to get most people out of the house, that was easy. Kenyon and I spent a few minutes walking around the oceanfront on Atlantic Avenue between 14th and 18th Streets, looking in the shops just like tourists. Sure enough, we quickly spotted two young black kids walking down the boardwalk, pants pulled down below their butt crack, Nikes unlaced, with the blue "do-rag" colors.

I yelled over to them, "Hey, how's your girlie boss's arm feeling?" They started toward us, when the larger of the kids held his friend back and started talking to him. They turned and made a bee-line toward 16th street. Reinforcements would be coming. We would be gone.

Julio saw the two men run into the duplex and in about 30 seconds eight of them scrambled out of the house, one man had a cast on his arm. They jumped into 2 cars and headed for the oceanfront, only 5 blocks away. One lookout was left behind, sitting on the steps, smoking a joint.

Julio entered the back door, slipping the lock with a pick.

He was perfectly still for 3 minutes, listening for the noise of others in the house. Things were quiet. The house was a shit hole. Pizza boxes and liquor bottles strewn around with plenty of empty beer cans. The place reeked of marijuana.

The gang had cut a doorway between the duplexes to allow for more room. OK, Julio thought, two attics. He went into the boarded up side first. That's the one he'd use. He found a scuttle ceiling access in one of the two bedrooms and pulled a chair over to stand on. He pushed up the 3x3 board covering the attic and looked around.

There it was. An old, wrinkled grocery bag about 3 feet from the access door. He pulled it over and looked inside. Bundles of money, all hundreds or fifties, wrapped in rubber bands. He quickly counted a stack of hundreds, $10,000, and it was exactly half the size of the stack of fifties, so each stack was ten grand. There were 25 stacks. He removed 2 bills from each stack, and stuck them in his pocket. That's all he needed. He put the rest of the money back inside the old bag, wrinkled the top closed, replaced the access door, moved the chair back and exited the back door locking it behind him.

Julio walked behind 4 other houses before reemerging on 16th street. His rented car was two blocks over on 18th. He drove down to the oceanfront and saw the spectacle of several young black men searching through the shops and fast food places, without any luck. Kenyon and Josh had rented two rooms at the Embassy Suites, just down the street, and were sitting on the balcony watching the ocean, drinking a Corona, along with Half Track.

Josh sensed someone behind him and turned quickly, only to see Julio. He had entered the room without anyone hearing.

"Dammit, Julio, you're going to get shot some day doing that."
"Doubtful," said Julio. Josh thought the man was probably right. Julio described his find. He had taken 2 bills from each stack. They now knew how many stacks there were in each denomination, they just needed the "filler".

Josh had spent the morning cashing American Express Traveler's checks at five different banks, getting 500 one dollar bills from each. The old trick of cutting up newspapers just didn't work. The paper weight was different, and looking from the side, you could tell that it was a fake.

Why take more chances than you had to? The four of them went to work putting 98 ones between 2 hundred dollar bills, and 198 ones between 2 fifties, then wrapping the stacks in rubber bands. They had bought a cheap gym satchel, so the "fake" stacks went in there. Packaging the fake bundles took about an hour.

Julio would double back to the duplex, sneak back in, and make the switch, putting the stuffed packs in the grocery sack and bring the real drug money stash back to the hotel. Julio left with the "package" and called Josh in five minutes saying he was in position, just down the street from the duplex.

Kenyon and Josh walked out the back, ocean side, of the hotel and went about three blocks south before coming out on Atlantic Avenue. Sure enough, in less than two minutes a boy with a blue do-rag was on his cell phone talking excitedly. The boy stayed put. He was obviously told not to lose the two men like they had done before.

Julio, once again saw the duplex empty out and head for the ocean to confront Josh and Kenyon. Julio slipped back in the same door as before.

As his training had taught, he waited 3 minutes, listening for any sounds in the house. Once again, there were none, just the "stoner" lookout on the front porch.

He slipped into the side bedroom, used the chair again, and put the "fake" money in the brown bag, wrinkled the top, and left with over $240,000 in drug "buy" money.

Josh went into a t-shirt shop and asked for the manager. A cute blonde in her early twenties, came out of the back. "I'm Erin," she said. "My Dad owns three of these shops, I manage this one." Josh started his tale, "Look, Erin, we're from out of town," he said pointing at Kenyon.

"This gang has been hassling us for the past two days, and they're threatening violence. I don't want to involve you, so we're going to walk across the street, but if you see them come at us, could you call the police? No one will know it's you," I assured her. "Are these the guys with the blue kerchiefs?" she asked. I nodded. "I'll be glad to call, they're in here threatening us and our customers all the time."

Kenyon and I walked across the street. We didn't have to wait long. The Navigator pulled up and Tyrell jumped out holding an aluminum baseball bat. "Well, if it isn't "ebony and ivory," he said.

"I thought you'd still be at home crying like a girl," I said. Tyrell looked back at his "homies." "Can you believe the mouth on this guy. You about to get busted up," he said. "You're going to need more people," Kenyon said. About that time, Half Track came out of the store behind us and stood beside Kenyon.

He created a large shadow. Tyrell looked like he had seen a ghost. One of the 'bangers got out of the second car, a gun stuck in his pants. Then, just as if on cue, two Virginia Beach police cruisers pulled up with lights rolling.

The gang member with the gun quickly pulled his shirt over it, hiding it from prying eyes.

"We got a call that there was trouble here," the officer questioned. I looked at my watch. Tyrell had been here for 8 minutes. Julio had been at the duplex for 9. I wanted 3-4 more minutes for safety. "No officer," I said, "my friend with the broken arm here was welcoming us to Virginia Beach."

The last thing Tyrell wanted, was to go down to the jail on "pick-up day." That was one thing we agreed on. I didn't want him arrested today either. "Besides that," I said pointing at Kenyon, "my friend was a SEAL stationed here, and he was just showing his old Marine buddy around."

At the mention of the word SEAL, Tyrell backed up a step or two. "Let them shake on it, and we'll be on our way."

Kenyon stuck out his right hand and gripped the hand extended from the cast. I'm sure he broke at least one finger, but Tyrell couldn't say a word. "Sorry to be a bother, officer," I said. The gang drove off. Fifteen minutes, plenty of time for Julio to make the switch. We walked back to the beach side of the hotels, checked for tails, and went back to our room. Julio was waiting there with a satchel full of money.

It was still only 4 pm. So we all had a Corona and met to decide how we would divide up the money. We got Milo on the speaker phone. Everyone had a vote.

Off the top, we decided to give $20,000 for college to Dante and Bonita, and also to Kenyon's youngest brother who was just entering college this year. It would be put in a trust, which uncle/brother Kenyon would manage.

Our expenses for the trip, airfare, cars, hotels, shotguns, and

$2500 in dollar bills, would be about $8,000. I had Kenyon go to the other room and call his father, Reverend White.

He came back about 5 minutes later. They've raised $23,000. The expansion will cost 50k. "Well Kenyon, I think we can all agree that construction almost always costs more than estimated. Will everyone agree to $30,000. We all nodded, Milo agreed on the speakerphone.

"You told him the terms, right, anonymous?" I asked Kenyon. "We negotiated. He wants to call the expansion the 'Special Wing', after 'Special Corps.' He said that's how he would remember our generosity...Special." I asked, "Anybody have a problem with that?" No one did.

"I'd like to put $20,000 into the company account, for any emergencies," I said. Everyone nodded again.

"So, we started with $246,000, minus $60,000 for the kids' college, 30k for the church, and 8 thousand for expenses, 20k for the company. That leaves $128,000. What's that divided by 5, Milo?" "Twenty five thousand, six hundred, apiece," he answered. I said, "OK, that's how I want it. We'll just call it a Christmas bonus. All in favor, say Aye," and the Ayes carried the day.

At the airport the next morning, Julio brought over today's edition of *The Virginian Pilot*, the local paper. On the front page of the *Hampton Roads* section was a photograph of a police crime scene.

A Black Lincoln Navigator was at the center. The headline read. "Three Dead in Gang Shootout, Police Suspect Drugs" The story continued below.

"Timothy Tyrell Jackson, and two yet to be identified men were found shot dead at the scene in a remote Virginia Beach location. Jackson had a string of previous drug arrests, and was identified at the scene by Virginia Beach Police. The police further stated that the other two victims were in Mr. Jackson's employ, and lived with him on 16th Street in Virginia Beach.

"Who would have thought he'd be killed trying to double cross another drug dealer?" volunteered Kenyon. "Well, nobody's going to miss him."

"Just Bonita and Dante," I said, "But in a good way."

It was going to be a great trip home.

Don't Mess With Jess

Jess Flowers' training program was almost concluded. She'd worked the first eighteen months of her internship exclusively in hotel management and the food/beverage operations. Now that she was 21, she could be involved in learning the casino side of the business. It was also important to her to be respected, and Jess was.

In her casino training, she alternated between working with people in the security center, and working alongside the personnel on the floor. In the security center they watched for cheats among the gamblers, and from the staff. They also had people who watched the "watchers". Her Dad had told her that every casino had "inside" people. The trick was finding them, proving that they were cheaters beyond any doubt, and then "throwing the book" at them, hoping to discourage any of those who were on the fence with their honesty. Polygraphs and mandatory drug tests helped, but like anything else, they could be beaten.

The most common method cheaters use is collusion with a dealer, usually at blackjack. That's why these tables are the most watched game by security. Her Dad depended on the security team and cameras (eyes in the sky) to spot them all. "They look for patterns, Jess", her father had told her. "If the dealer looks at his hole card a microsecond longer than he usually does, if he's noticed with the same players at his back, sitting at a different table, on more than a single occasion, if he buys a boat or has a kid hooked on meth, he's a suspect.

And our security personnel suspects everyone, even me and you, Jess," he belabored, "but that's their job." You don't see them at the holiday Christmas party, do you?" he asked. "But if it weren't for them, we wouldn't have our jobs."

Jess enjoyed working with the security staff, but the real action was out on the "floor". She didn't make decisions, yet, she just observed, and learned. One of the first things she had done was to learn the "games." Blackjack, poker, and roulette, had been fairly easy. The larger hotels, like the "Beau Rivage", had free gaming classes for guests, and Jess had sat through most of them, twice.

The slots she had always thought of as no brainers, but then she learned that there were people who attempted to use magnets, or other devices to manipulate the random outcome. She had been assigned to work with floor personnel in the slots, several times. Jess had worked her way up through slots, roulette, and was about to take on the most complex game, craps.

Craps was a whole different environment. She had to learn the terminology like "the hard (or easy) way", "yo", "press", "come", "pass", and even the most simplistic ones like "snake eyes" and "boxcars". On top of that, it was very important where and when a bet was placed.

A craps table is so complicated, that there are three or four personnel assigned to each table. These included (1) the "stick man" (or woman), who is in charge of the dice, they use a curved stick, and announce the game. Then (2) the "box man" who oversees the table, and handles the chips, makes change, etc. At the higher stakes tables, there are sometimes two "box men".

Finally there is (3) the "dealer" whose job it is to place the bets, and keep the game moving. The casinos know that the more rolls they get per table, the more money they make...it's all in the odds. Looking over the shoulder of the table staff are the floor persons, who usually handle two or three tables each, and report to the pit boss.

The game itself is chaotic. Lots of motion, plenty to see, and when someone starts rolling numbers, it turns into a mixture of The Roman Coliseum and The Super Bowl.

The most popular method for cheating at craps, is using loaded dice. That is, dice which are weighted, or hollowed out to make it marginally more probable to roll certain numbers. But, it's almost impossible to get counterfeit dice into a game. Even if you have assistance from one of the employees at the table, there are several others who are watching him.

Plus, the dice are changed frequently, at random times, for no apparent reason. There are several times when an entire group of dice are eliminated from the game. A die gets thrown off the table and hits the floor, change them out. Dice disappear in someone's hands for a fraction of a second, change them out.

This was Friday night, and Jess was going to observe a floor person in one of the pits. This was her first time to stand behind the velvet ropes, watching two craps tables. Floor persons and pit bosses wear a sports coat. Jess had bought two from "The Edge" for just such occasions.

About 9:30 a "shooter" (the person rolling the dice at the time) got hot. He was playing the numbers 6 and 8. Three times in a row, he hit one of these two numbers, and he just kept "letting it ride." The shooter was about 50 years old, about 50 pounds overweight, and slightly inebriated. He was putting on quite a show, letting his companion, a woman half his age, blow on the dice before each role. After a couple of inconsequential rolls, he put a $1,000 chip on a "hard eight" (each die coming up with a 4), and he hit it, a 9 to 1 winner, he won the $9,000, and "let it ride" again which meant that including his original bet, he had $10,000 on the hard eight,

Bet, a payout of $90,000. Jess was hearing noise from another table, but it wasn't in her pit, so she ignored it. And then it happened.

The shooter's girl friend leaned over to blow on the chips, a neighboring player bumped her and one of the die stuck to her lipstick heavy upper lip. She quickly brushed it off, the die landing on the floor. The shooter picked them up. Jess looked for her floor person, but he was not there, he was at another table.

"New dice," Jess asserted.

"No way," responded the shooter. "These are my lucky dice and I'm not giving them up," he stated boldly.

"New dice," Jess said, with even more conviction. "They hit the floor, new dice!" Jess ordered, staring at the stickman. "I want the boss, these are my dice," the shooter said.

Just then, Jess heard a loud voice directly behind her. "New dice." It was Timmy Roland, the head pit boss of the entire casino. "I say new dice," he stared at the shooter, "and I'm the boss. Something else you want to talk to me about?"

Tommy offered the shooter two choices, "You can get new dice and roll, or you can collect your bets and leave the table, which may be the best odds you get tonight. Pick one, now."

The shooter hesitated, then gave the dice to the stick man, who pushed a new group of dice toward the shooter for him to select from.

A little less booze, and no young girlfriend, odds are he would have walked away with his winnings. He was trapped. He picked two new dice and rolled... "snake eyes, loser," announced the stickman. Jess stared at the table with no outward emotion. But inside, she was shaking. Timmy Roland took her to the side and said, "Congratulations. A lot of rookies would have caved in there, but you held your ground and were right to do so. You can work in my pit anytime."

Jess' shift ended without any further controversy. She had a lot to think about on the short drive home. After tonight she knew she "belonged." And word would get around.

Fall Swings

October was the best time to be in the deep south. The hot, ragged edge of summer along with the constant high humidity, had abated and most days were in the 70s. The hurricane season was almost past, and though we officially had a few more weeks, it appeared that the Gulf Coast had been spared this year.

Football was in full swing, however the Saints had stumbled to an 0-4 start after a promising 10-6 record the year before. The rabid fan base was screaming for blood, but the team had been disappointing for most of their 41 year existence.

Josh's company had completed a 4 day job for the NBA in late September. It was a 4-day mini-camp at the coliseum. There wasn't much to it. Their main goal had been to control the "groupies" and keep the players from hurting each other. Guys who average 6'8", 285, don't get mugged very often.

Many wives and children attended for moral support, and to keep their men under control. Most of these guys were mid-level, early in their careers, or rookie players, but there was still a large contingent of girls trying to land a potential multi-millionaire as a boyfriend or husband.

The next job for "Special Corps" started next week. It was not a huge job either. The PGA "Champions Tour" (formerly the Senior Tour) was having a tournament at the new, Tom Fazio designed "Fallen Oak Golf Course", conveniently, only about 20 miles away, in the small town of Saucier, Mississippi.

The course had a exclusive affiliation with the "Beau Rivage Hotel and Casino", so most of the golfers would be staying there.

There would be the usual PGA security, however this year was special as this was the initial year of eligibility for Fred Anders, who was an immensely popular golfer.

Kenny Plum and Leonard Ware, past winners of the "Player of the Year" had also registered, so much larger crowds than ordinary were expected. Special Corps had been asked to focus on these three players. Also, with ESPN televising the event, the "Tour" wanted additional help.

The town of Saucier was too small to handle any additional security, so Special Corps had been hired to augment the protection.

The golfers would come in on Tuesday, have a practice round on Wednesday, and a "Pro-Am" on Thursday, with several of the corporate sponsors.

Josh pared his team down to Kenyon, Julio, and himself, as he knew that Half Track would stand out in a crowd. Golfers, and their fans were not usually large people. He would use him and Milo as back-up, if needed.

The golfers would complete the 3 day (as opposed to the regular tour's 4 day) tournament on Sunday. There was no "cut". Everyone who played, finished the tournament. Most of them would leave on Monday for the next event. Almost all of them owned or leased time on private planes.

Tuesday came and the three members of "Special Corps" were at the golf course awaiting the arrival of their three important guests.

All the golf pros' clothes, clubs, and gear had been taken to the "Beau Rivage", or other hotels via separate vehicles.

Limos with police escorts brought the pros to this beautiful course. We had picked names out of a hat. Josh had drawn Fred Anders, and Kenny Plum's name was picked by Kenyon, which left Julio with Leonard Ware, a previous major championship winner.

As it turned out, each of these men was most gracious, respectful, and fan friendly. I had always heard, and now witnessed, that the largest winners on the PGA tour, were the charities. Half of the money from this tournament would go to build houses and shelters for those impacted by Katrina.

The other half would go to the V.A. hospital in Biloxi. In fact, after a short, registration and get acquainted ceremony in the clubhouse, all three of our golfers, and several others, had a 3:00 tour of the V.A. hospital on their agenda.

The hotel had 6 extra limos to take the golfers to the course, the V.A. hospital, and back to the hotel. They would be delivering them to the course and back every day as well.

As luck would have it, all three of our assignments arrived within 45 minutes of each other. Leonard Ware was the first to arrive. The PGA advance man introduced us all to Mr. Ware, who was warm and welcoming. "Nice of you folks to worry about me," he said. Josh said, "Welcome to Mississippi, Mr. Ware."

"Mr. Ware, I added, "Our job is to protect you in a such a way that you don't even notice us, and to make sure you have nothing to worry about except golf. We know that you do this for yourself, and for charity."

I knew he had his own charity work and foundation. I told him that he was lucky, Julio, an ex-green beret had been personally assigned to him, and if he had any concerns, Julio was the man.

Anders and Plum arrived shortly thereafter, and their reception, courtesy, and hospitality was equally as good. In fact, after the introductions the first thing Plum asked was, "When do we get to go to the hospital?" like it was a big treat for them.

"Right after registration," said the PGA official. About 2:45, two dozen golfers (many of them, millionaires) were eagerly awaiting their trip to the hospital, to quote Anders, "This is where we meet the real heroes." We rode along.

The administrator of the facility met us in the foyer. He said, "This is more people than I expected. A lot more, but we're very proud that you've taken time out to spend a few minutes with some of our Veterans.

"I know a lot of you guys have hectic travel schedules, both here and abroad. Once you devote some time with your families, it's amazing to me that you have any time left for things like this."

"We've got plenty left," said Craig Taylor, another, former Champions Tour 'Player of the Year'. Plenty for the golf course, and plenty for our wounded men and women in uniform." And with that, a big applause broke out among the surrounding staff, the golfers, and the members of Special Corps.

"Well," the VA administrator continued," we have three basic groups of severely wounded or ill veterans, here. I've not taken the liberty to divide how many ever there are of you into 3 groups, you get to pick where you go, but please, not all to the same place.

I've got the amputee rehab center, the severe burn trauma unit, and the palliative care facility. Volunteers?"

Fred Anders volunteered to lead the group into the burn trauma unit.

He had a friend who was badly injured in a fire, and wanted to share his successful recovery story with the patients.

Kenny Plum picked the toughest one, palliative care...end of life planning. He was a devout Christian, and wanted to be with those for whom there was no hope. Leonard Ware had a relative who had a 6 handicap, even with an artificial leg, so he picked the rehab center. The visit lasted over an hour.

Only when the administrator insisted on rest for his patients, were they able to get the golfers to leave.

There were plenty of teary eyes on the way back to the hotel. But, they had brought a little sunshine, and some hope, into people's lives, who were starved for both. Back at the hotel, the golfers went to their rooms to get ready for a dinner with some of the major sponsors.

We three went to the dinner, but I sat at the back of the room, with Kenyon and Julio outside the lobby of the restaurant the PGA had reserved for tonight.

It was strictly "by invitation only." a couple of autograph seekers approached the hostess, who cued Kenyon to cut them off at the door. Nothing rough, it was just a private dinner. One man told the hostess he had forgotten his invitation.

Julio went to the PGA official and it was quickly determined that he was a photographer, trying to get some inside shots. We quickly sent him on his way. Maybe I could have used Half Track.

I had arranged to get our three golf professionals into adjacent rooms, and secured a room for us across the hall.

That way the three of us could rotate sentry duty throughout the night.

We didn't expect this assignment to be much more than a routine babysitting job. After all, these guys were all over 50 years old, most of them had grandkids.

The next day Plum and Anders were off to the course for their early morning practice round. They were playing together, so Kenyon and I got to spend the day seeing the game as it was supposed to be played. We had both tried golf Kenyon usually scored in the high 80s to low 90s...much better than me, but this was different. We would ride in separate golf carts and follow our assigned pro, but we always met up on the tee boxes, and the greens.

On the first tee, we found out how humbled we were going to feel. Kenny Plum was 5'8", 165 pounds. The first hole is a long par 5, dogleg left, almost 600 yards long. Plum took out his driver and ripped his tee shot right down the middle, 295 yards away. Kenyon looked at me, and we both just shook our heads and smiled. This was a game with which we were not familiar.

The rest of the round was more of the same. To quote the PGA slogan, "These Guys Are Good!"

The next day was entertaining. Persons who had lofty positions with some of the corporations who were sponsors of the event were able to rub elbows and share the round with these pros. The sponsors used the forward tees, and occasionally were given individual tips on their game from the experts.

None of our pros' teams were in the running. The corporate sponsors who were with the pros we were with, were really "hackers", who just happened to own a set of clubs.

One of our sponsors actually made a par on the third hole, a par 3, but it was downhill from there.

On the 12th hole, Leonard Ware, accompanied by Julio, was getting ready for his birdie putt, when a man ducked under the ropes and headed across the green in their direction. Julio, turned quickly, and heard the man yelling "murderer, butcher" at one of the VIP playing sponsors.

His target, Leonard Ware's partner in the event, was the president of a regional meat packing plant in Birmingham.

The "fan" ran toward the sponsor with a jar of what looked like blood, which he was intending to throw on the sponsor, all the time calling him a "murderer".

Julio ran to the intruder, and with a classic "clothesline" (extended arm across the neck) tackle, took the attacker down, hard, and Julio handcuffed him immediately.

The man was still gasping for breath when a State Trooper got there about a minute later, and took the culprit away.

The crowd around the green gave Julio a standing ovation, with cheers and hoots. He was a little embarrassed. The crowd quieted down quickly, and fittingly, Ware made his birdie putt.

Julio called Josh and told him that everything was under control. Even better, since it was a pro-am event, and not actually part of the tournament, ESPN had missed the incident.

The VIP/sponsor thanked Julio profusely, offering to pay him directly. "No," Julio replied, "I'm getting paid already, I'm just doing my job."

That night the team received an update from the State Police. The perpetrator was a leader in one of the animal rights groups who believed that no one should eat meat, eggs, milk, or wear leather shoes or belts. The intended victim had decided against pressing charges, and the publicity was kept to a minimum.

That's exactly what organizations like this thrive on. Don't want to give them any ammunition or martyrs. The PGA agreed with the decision.

The whole team knew, that there is nothing more dangerous than a zealot. Give someone a cause, any cause, and they would do irrational things.

Tomorrow was Friday, the opening day of the tournament. The crowds were good, but would get better on the weekend. The day was beautiful, despite a 60 minute fog delay in the morning. The pros teed off beginning at 10:30, and you could tell that now, this was work.

Their eyes narrowed and demeanors changed, all trying to stay within the moment. All focusing on one shot at a time.

No less a golf legend than Bobby Jones once proclaimed that "Golf is a game played on a 5 inch course...the distance between your ears."

Being out here, Josh could see the truth in that observation. He'd seen plenty of athletes in his life. Great basketball players, but only one Michael Jordan, great baseball pitchers, but Nolan Ryan was the master. With all the exceptional, once in a generation, stars you could see it in their eyes.

In tough situations, they wanted the ball, they cherished the responsibility and the challenge.

Saturday and Sunday came and went, without incident. The crowds were large, but respectful. Golf is still a "gentleman's game," (no disrespect to the LPGA, Josh was a huge Annika Sorenstam fan) where players followed certain behaviors, and actually called penalties on themselves.

On Sunday, Kenyon's pro, Kenny Plum, won the tournament and $140,000, by sinking a 22 foot putt on the second playoff hole.

However, as at all PGA Tournaments, charity was the big winner. During the awards ceremony, The Katrina homeless fund, and the Veteran's Hospital, each received a check for $250,000 from the PGA of America. Life was made a little better for those less fortunate.

Real Estate Slumps

Connie was committed to the real estate career she had started a couple of years ago. Even the first year she had produced positive income, and was #6 in her 8 person office. Year two she had been #3. she had given herself a 4-year time–frame to make to the top, and be self-dependent.

Now the market was beginning to slow. It was time for her to kick it into high gear. Being a newer agent, she didn't have a list of client's who many of the veterans in her office had accumulated over the past 10 or 20 years. She would simply have to work harder.

Post cards, open houses, calling sellers whose listings had expired, contacting FSBO's, social networking, she couldn't leave any stone unturned.

The slowing market was caused by myriad reasons. Start with several years of home values rising at unsustainable rates. Then add undocumented loans, most importantly, add hundreds of thousands of sub-prime loans mandated by Congress to special groups of Americans who had extremely poor credit scores, and finally, pile on rampant speculation by builders and investors.

The net result was that foreclosures were way up, and despite very low interest rates, sales were way down.

She was determined to give it 100%. Connie was now holding open houses on every Sunday, 2-4, mailing her quota of 100 post cards a month, and forcing herself to make a minimum of 2 calls per day to eligible sellers such as FSBOs and expired listings.

It had helped her make one sale transaction last month, and acquire a listing, which may sell or not. This was real estate.

You pay hundreds of dollars a year in real estate and MLS fees, you spend money for the best equipment, cell phones, computers, laptops, pda's, cars, gas, advertising and, yard signs. Along with that you give prospective "buyers", tours of homes, and after two or three afternoons of doing this, some of them wouldn't return your calls.

They just wanted to learn the market, so they can go buy a home without a realtor, hoping to get a lower price. This usually doesn't work. The listing agent gets all the broker fees, which would have been split, and the buyer doesn't have anyone representing them, in the biggest transaction of their life.

Finding a home you like is the easy part. Then what about the fair price for a similar property in this neighborhood? You have to look at comparable sales, not just what someone said he sold for next door. How do you shop for the best financing? People who couldn't, or wouldn't teach their own kids to read, would go out in the world and spend $2-$300,000, without knowing about title defects, mechanic's liens, lead paint, home inspectors, and now, Chinese drywall.

Also, it's the buyer's real estate agent who was supposed to investigate surrounding properties. Was a sewage treatment plant going in across the street? Was a new road planned just behind the house? There were literally hundreds of ways you make a bad investment in a home, but most of these are easily avoidable by using a professional to assist you.

Connie knew all these things and was up-to-date on all the State and Government regulations.

She was good at being there to find the right home, and offer her opinion, once they narrowed down the selection.

After that, writing a purchase agreement and negotiating the business terms of the agreement were things which she was very good at, as well.

Once the agreement had been ratified by all parties, she would see to it that her clients received the best, possible assistance from a host of professionals. To avoid any hint of favoritism, She had a list of "professional service experts" she gave to each client. At the top of the list in bold print was typed. "Below is a list of service providers utilized by prior clients of mine. You can use them or select your own."

And then she gave her clients the names of at least three providers in each category:

Home Inspectors
Attorneys
Lenders
Termite-Moisture Inspectors
Title Companies
Homeowners Insurance
Moving Companies

After that, she had the names and phone numbers of the utility companies, cable, and telephone services.

Yes, Connie had turned into a real pro, but the market was definitely a bear. And Connie was always prepared for changes. It comes with the territory.

Hold 'Em

The entire country was buzzing about the latest sports phenomena, "Texas Hold 'Em" poker tournaments. The "Beau Rivage" was not going to let this opportunity pass them by. It was right up their alley. Entire "Hold Em" tours were developing around the country, no, around the world. The Bellagio had considerable success in their first tournament, held only a few years ago. Hold Em's phenomenal growth had been attributed to the "Moneymaker effect."

In 2003. Chris Moneymaker, an accountant who was going through a divorce at the time, invested $40 in an on-line poker tournament. He won the tournament, and most importantly won a seat at the WSOP (World Series of Poker). At that event, he beat a seasoned pro, Sam Farha, and won $2.5 million dollars. Since that time, several other "on-line" players have had success at tournaments around the world.

Now, the "Beau Rivage" was going to be an annual stop for the newest, nationally sponsored poker tourney, named "Journey to the Top". This tour would hold seven events leading up to the finale in Las Vegas. How the players fared in these preliminary events would determine the size of their starting chip stack at the final "Grand Event."

This exclusive tournament would start in Vegas, then Atlantic City, Nassau, Aruba, Biloxi, New Orleans, and end up back in Las Vegas, with the major Vegas casinos rotating to be the beginning and finish of the "Grand Event."

The sponsors were aiming to be more exclusive than the WSOP, where thousands lined up to play. They would begin with 240 players.

With 240 players, it was thought that the promoters could line up some of the world's best, possibly Phil Ivey, Doyle Brunson, Johnny Chan, etc. All veteran pros with high name recognition from "The World Series of Poker."

They would still have plenty of room for the celebrity players, Hollywood actors and sports stars, and round out the field by including the best foreign players.

The "field" would originally contain 240 players, mainly pros, but also several "on-line wonders." It would be cut by 20% at each event, with the top 80% going on to the next tournament. The participants would number 240, 192, 154, 123, 98, 78, with the final 62 players making it to the Las Vegas, 2-day Finale. There would be 2 weeks between stops.

One simple reason for the time spread was to give ample opportunity for the network to hype the next event.

The second reason was to allow the pros to make some real money in the "high stakes rooms" of the casinos, beating the ever present "poker idiot" who had lots of money but wanted to try his luck sitting across from pros like Johnny Chan, winner of multiple WSOP bracelets. Well, these guys are good, too. But there were plenty of suckers born every minute.

The "Beau Rivage", in 5th position, out of the 7 sites, would host 98 players. This meant huge crowds for the 2-day event, extra exposure for the hotel, network TV, extensive media coverage, and additional headaches for the hotel, and its' staff. The word was that next year's stop would be at the nearby "Hard Rock Hotel and Casino."

Special Corps, won the added security job over 3 other firms, including "Viper Security" (Butch Wingo) Josh's local competition. The out of towners had no strong desire for a 2 or 3 day gig. It was too small for them.

Also, "Viper", was in the midst of a State investigation for receiving stolen property. They had always operated barely within the law. This time they may have crossed the line.

This made Josh's company an easy choice. Since his Dad was the assistant G.M. for the hotel, every effort was made to show that 'Special Corps' selection had been above board. The hotel had taken out ads, asking for bids on the job in the New Orleans, Mobile, Jackson, and Atlanta newspapers, as well as the local, *Sun Herald*. Special Corps was awarded the job about 60 days prior to the tournament.

Josh's job was not to look for people "running a game" or counting cards, the "Beau Rivage" had experts who knew the cheating business, inside and out. Josh knew MGM Resorts International, the owners, had brought in specialists from their other casino properties, solely to help with this task.

It was guaranteed that the results would be legitimate. They didn't have to look too closely at the top pros. These people lived and died as a direct result of their prowess at the casinos.

Any hint of cheating would immediately ban them from casinos, worldwide. It was the on-line and "wanna-be" players who would draw the scrutiny of the "watchers", and their dozens of concealed cameras. Each of these also attracted very intense scrutiny, and background checks by Milo, Special Corps computer research employee (think, 'hacker').

The job of Special Corps was twofold. First, the casino had transformed two of it's private gambling rooms into "High Limit" tables (they usually had only one). In order to play you had to either (a) be on the 98 person tourney list, or (b) register 72 hours in advance, depositing the mandatory table limit of the particular room, either $5,000 or $10,000, with the hotel at the same time.

This is where Half Track, and Julio, would be stationed. One of them would be in each of the "High Limit" rooms.

They were to wear sports coats (60 xxl for "Track"), and not brandish, but also not hide their licensed firearms. Sore losers were the largest threat.

They would be relieved in 8-hour shifts by Drake and Pete, two highly respected investigators who had helped Josh on jobs in the past. Most recently with Holly Santa Cruz.

Secondly, Josh and Kenyon were to provide backup security on the 3 floors, 8, 9, and 10, which the hotel had blocked out for the tournament invitees. There were 3 Biloxi Police Officers on each floor.

One officer each, was stationed by the 2 stair well doors. These had to remain unlocked due to the fire codes, and the third cop being beside the elevators. Josh and Kenyon knew most of the officers. Their job was to patrol the floors, randomly, also in 8 hour shifts.

No one was to come to these floors without being registered here. If one of the players picked up a "date" they went elsewhere.

Bringing children to the tournament was also strongly discouraged. They couldn't be in the casino area, or the bars, what was the point? Thursday was check in day. Friday and Saturday were tournament dates, Most players would check out of the hotel Saturday night, Sunday morning, or when eliminated.

At the hotel, everything was in place by Thursday at 10 am. The field was now down to 96 players. An NCIC check, instigated by Milo's discovery of false id's, had found that two invitees had prior felony convictions, a big no-no for entry.

Players in Limos started drifting in from Aruba, Las Vegas and Atlantic City, where many of the pros lived, and points in between.

The mandatory, post-registration meeting was to be at 2 pm. It was at that time that the tournament rules would be discussed, and the players would be introduced to hotel executives, Police Chief Holmes, and Josh's 6-man crew, excluding Milo.

The meeting was in the "Theatre" and the players, spouses, friends, managers, and other personnel were drifting in starting at 1:55. This was not an early group. The tournament rules were identical to the previous events, but the people who provided hotel services, dinner and driver reservations, and security, were all different.

The rules for behavior were simple. Any player's guests who did not behave properly, were banned from the premises. Security was with you on the hotel/casino property, only. You want to go out and start flashing cash, take your chances.

Some of the pros carried large sums of money with them, but the better known pros had huge credit lines they could draw on, and didn't, need cash. After meeting and being welcomed by Messrs. Rutland and Tom Flowers, hotel security, then Chief Holmes, Josh introduced his staff to the group. He could already see money being wagered on the "side" as to the weight of "Track". These guys would bet on anything.

This initiated a serious discussion on when the "weigh-in"

would be held, and it was agreed that scales would be brought into the "Theatre", immediately after the meeting. Mr. Rutland would send a bell boy for 2 of them. Three hundred twenty eight, and a half pounds, was the winner.

The rest of Thursday appeared to be routine. Both high stakes rooms were full of contestants and fat catters ready to give their money to some well-known pro, just to say they played with them. Traffic was light on the floors.

Kenyon had a strange scene develop during one of his shifts on the three floors. One, obviously drunk, man had somehow gotten off on what was the wrong floor, (9) arguing with the police that this was his floor.

They checked the desk, and he was a registered guest, but his room was 3 floors below. How had his keycard worked to access this "blocked off" floor? We called hotel security immediately. The cops were laughing about the drunk. We weren't so sure.

Later that night, Kenyon and I walked the halls together, talking about scenarios. While hotel operations and security people were pointing fingers at each other, I made a call to Milo, asking him to deliver some "contingency equipment."

Down in the high stakes rooms, sheep were being shorn and all was right with the world. A modestly inebriated man was playing a different version of "Hold 'Em", called "Omaha", and accused another (non-pro) of trying to view his hole cards.

The man had insinuated the same accusation earlier in the evening. Now he had a little more Scotch in him and he pointed at an opponent and said "cheater."

Half Track assisted the regular hotel security in cashing the player out, and removing the man from the building. The "High Stakes" room got back to normal, but witnesses saw that unruly behavior would be dealt with, immediately.

It was important to establish the ground rules as early as possible. Casinos have reputations and perceptions from their customers. The "Beau Rivage" wanted, like all others, to be seen as honest, fair, but would not allow bar fights or shouting matches.

The Tournament

Friday was finally here, and we were prepared for all possibilities, we thought. Thursday had been a dry run, and helped us become more familiar with personalities.

The games began at 1 pm, in the "Theatre", although the sports network broadcast would be taped, edited, and shown beginning at 8 pm that night. A three hour show Friday night, and another of the same length on Saturday night. What, you thought these things just happened to climax just in time for the next scheduled program?

If all went according to plan, the initial day of the 2-day event would end around 4-5 pm, and those remaining could get a little rest (or not), and report back at 1 pm tomorrow.

The announcer spoke excitedly into his microphone, "Shuffle Up and Deal" and the tournament was on. Friends, traveling companions, and spouses had two viewing choices. They could sit in the small 6-row high bleachers, close (but not close enough to see any cards) or they could watch, on closed circuit TV, from the "The Players' Club", with the ability to see the hole card, odds, and betting strategies.

Once in the TV room, however, you could not leave until that day's 3-4 hours of gambling was over, even if your player was knocked out early. And cell phones were prohibited. This was to prevent the passing of information such as "player X has been bluffing player Y, all night." Even if you were traveling with player Z. If you had to go to the bathroom, you had a security person, usually one of Josh's, go with you.

The first night actually came to a good place to end at about 4:45. The players almost always played conservatively in the beginning, not wanting to be eliminated too quickly.

There had been 10 eliminations, which left 8 tables of 10 players and 1 table with 6, for the championship.

The tournament play was officially suspended for the day, with some players headed to the high stakes rooms, some to an early dinner, a very few, back to their rooms.

Josh and his men had actually been able to rest during the tournament, with all eyes focused on the tables, there wasn't much to do. The police were on the 3 secured floors, and there wasn't much action in the "High Stakes" rooms...not with the best in the world playing just across the casino floor.

His men resumed their posts, "Track" and Julio in the "High Stakes" rooms, Kenyon and Josh back to their upstairs floors which were blocked off. They made the first trip around the floors together, letting the Police know that play had stopped for the day, but they had been told that already on their radios. Everyone seemed to have their focus, and were looking for a quiet night, maybe dealing with the occasional drunk.

WRONG! I'm not sure when the first fire alarm went off, but it couldn't have been much after 5:30 pm. It was immediately followed by two more alarms and intercom announcements to evacuate the building via the stairs, do not use the elevators, this is not a drill!

Josh looked at Kenyon, this is it. These 3 floors were almost deserted already, everyone was downstairs, and couldn't get back up to their rooms, clothes, jewelry, and in many cases, cash. Downstairs, some of the pros were banging on the lobby elevator doors, screaming that they must get back to their rooms. The police, and the elevators, wouldn't budge.

Black smoke started coming out of the HVAC vents.

Kenyon and I grabbed the bag which Milo had brought us today, and we quickly donned the SCBA oxygen tanks, and the clear goggles. We agreed, I'd go to 10, Kenyon to 8, and we'd meet on 9. Outside, we saw that the police were gone.

They weren't cowards, but they didn't have the protective equipment we had. I took the stairs up, he went down. Once on the floor we checked every room with our passkeys.

"All clear on 8," Kenyon barked through the radio. "Same here," I confirmed. The 9th floor was a different story. Three guys with gasmasks and axes were breaking into rooms, while a 4th was dumping cash and jewelry into large nap sacks.

"Freeze," I yelled, and squeezed a 9mm round out of my Glock into a nearby wall for extra emphasis, as the men ducked into a room. It had all been a diversion, probably scouted out by the "drunk" from the previous night. He had wanted to see the set-up. The would-be burglars had probably hidden in the stairwells or in a vacant room.

We had the 4 men between us. They weren't going anywhere. I called downstairs on my cell. Dad picked up right away. "Dad, it's a trick to rob the rooms I said."

"How do you know?" He yelled into the phone over the crowd. "One," I said, "I'm up here on 9, watching them do it. We have them trapped in a room," I added, "Two, if it was real, the robbers wouldn't take the risk of burning themselves up."

I continued, "There's either smoke being created in the kitchen, or more likely, the mechanical room has a 'smoke machine' hooked into the ventilator, making it look like a fire."

"Check out the mechanicals first," I said. "I'll let you know, he replied." Then Dad gave one of the smartest, or dumbest orders in his life. He called security, "Do not engage the sprinkler system. I repeat, do not allow the sprinklers to deploy. I want security on those water supply lines. Turn them off."

Then he called engineering and got them to the mechanical room. In five minutes Josh's hunch was confirmed. It was a diversion. A diversion which almost worked. The smoke began dissipating, almost immediately.

Josh heard the whir of the elevators come to life. And eight uniformed police personnel emptied out of the car, into the hall. Josh waved them over.

He didn't know if the robbers were armed, besides the axes, but figured they would not be. Most burglars are smart enough not to add felony gun possession, or attempted murder, to a common attempted robbery charge.

The police gave the order to surrender, and the culprits were smart enough to see that there was no way out. They backed out into the hallway, fingers locked over their heads. Kenyon recognized the "drunk" from last night, and pointed him out. The police were cuffing them and searching for weapons, finding none.

The last man out into the hall turned around and just looked at the floor. It was Josh's old pal, Butch Wingo, owner of "Viper Security." He was done.

After getting things back to normal, the hotel operations routine resumed just like it had never stopped. People were allowed back to their rooms.

Josh and Kenyon had stopped the looting early in the process, with only 3 rooms having been breached prior to cornering the robbers. The police let the three occupants sort out what belonged to who, in the nap sacks. It went pretty smoothly, and the victims agreed.

The local and sports TV media had been told that one of the HVAC compressors had failed, sending smoke and a false alarm through the building. They bought that cover, and everyone, including the tournament sponsors, were relieved. The tournament finished that Saturday, with no further interruptions or dramatics involved.

Most of the players left Sunday morning and Josh's responsibilities ended at check-out time, 10 am, that day. A few stragglers stayed to clean out some more "wanna bees", but most were off to New Orleans, via Vegas or Atlantic City.

Tom Flowers received a personal call from the CEO of MGM International. He praised Tom's insight into the situation. If the sprinklers had come on, there would have been millions of dollars in water damage to the hotel, plus lost revenues for 3-4 months. A nice bonus check would be in the mail.

Not to be forgotten, Special Corps also received a bonus, doubling their original fee. It was going to be a nice Holiday season.

Jess Flowers couldn't wait to hear the whole story. Rumors were flying through the hotel. She didn't know if she'd get the whole truth, but she wouldn't hear a lie out of Josh.

Mad Max, and Doris

The Sunday dinner was on. As much as Josh wanted to take the day off, he knew that his sisters counted on him for a break from Grandma and Max. The girls barely tolerated the old people as it was, and Josh always had fun with them and Goldie.

Josh, the girls, and Goldie were down at the dock, when the Lincoln Town Car, containing Doris and Max pulled into the driveway.

Josh and his sisters looked at the small John boat tied up to the dock only a few feet away. It was tempting to jump in the boat with Goldie, and paddle away from the dock for a couple of hours. Late fall breezes, the bay as smooth as glass, a light blue sky...no, never mind.

The four of them trudged back to the house ready to face the music of another Sunday with the octogenarians. It was impossible to escape anyway. Jess was preparing the meal.

"I promise, we'll have a talk, today, before I leave," Josh told the girls. He knew that they both wanted the inside "scoop" on the Poker Tournament.

They entered the house, "Oh we didn't hear you drive up," said Jess, (The Lincoln sounds like an Abrams Tank, Josh thought, how could you sneak up on anyone?).

"Well, we're here," replied a "snockered" Doris, "more or less." Princess ran under the dining room table. Doris had a way of stepping on her tail, if the cat wasn't alert.

Jess and Connie escaped to the kitchen, Josh, his Dad, and Goldie went to watch the football pre-game, which left Karen holding down the fort. Of course, Doris wanted to smoke one of her cheroot stogies, and have some more wine, so she went immediately to the back screened porch.

That left Max and Karen looking across the dining room table at each other. "I need to talk to you, Karen," Max said, it's about Doris." She wasn't going to get drawn into this, alone. "Tom, can you come in here for a moment, please?" Karen heard a moan, and a minute later, Tom walked in and sat at the table. "Max wants to talk about Mom," Karen said.

Max was dressed in another of his weird combinations. His wardrobe, today, was lime green double-knit slacks, light blue shirt, an orange cardigan sweater and the "full Cleveland" white patent shoes and belt. Add to that, a small wisp of white hair. However, today he looked helpless.

"She drinks constantly, all she wants is to drink wine, pass out, wake up, drink more wine, and pass out again. And, I don't even know how many cigars she smokes. Hell, even our sex is down to 3 or 4 times a week," he complained. Karen turned red, and changed the subject back to the drinking.

Karen said, "Max, you knew what she was before you moved in together. She's been like this for years. What would you like us to do? She won't listen to me, or Tom."

"I'm at a loss," he admitted. "I was hoping you would have some ideas." He seemed pitiful. "Let me give it some thought. I may have an angle on this which will make her think about her behavior," Karen added. Karen went out to the porch to check on Doris, and found her passed out in the chair, again.

Jess came out of the kitchen and told her Mom that the lamb chops, potatoes au gratin, and green beans would be ready in about 5 minutes. It was time to open the wine. Karen did have an idea.

"Lets just let her sleep through the dinner," Karen said. "When she wakes up, and we're through eating, we'll just say that she wouldn't 'come around'. A few embarrassments like that, might make her more responsible. We shouldn't be playing the role of enablers."

Karen added, "As long as she is protected from herself, and misses no meals, she'll go on like this until she kills herself."

Max liked the idea, and everyone sat at the table and ate, except Doris, sleeping on the porch.

After dinner, dessert was served...old-fashioned banana pudding, one of Doris' favorites, however, she was still passed out on the porch. When she finally awoke at 4 pm, and came inside, Karen told her that they were out of wine, and dessert was gone. Doris was fuming...but she only had herself to blame.

She tried to chastise Max, but he deferred, saying that she wouldn't wake up, what were they to do, not serve dinner to the entire family until she decided to "awaken?"

Tom, Josh, Goldie, and even Princess were in the family room watching game 2 of he NFL doubleheader. Doris kept complaining about being "left out", but no one was listening to her.

Finally, Max and Doris got ready to leave. Karen pulled Max to the side, and said, "It's just a beginning, don't give in. She's in quicksand, but you can't do this for her, she'll just pull you in and you'll both go under. She has to help herself."

They drove off in the Lincoln, and finally the family exhaled a breath of air, relieved they didn't have to face another rant from Doris about her exclusion.

Josh looked at his sisters, and nodded toward the dock. "Dad," he said, "we're taking Goldie for a walk, we'll be back in a few minutes," he said as they walked out the door. Down at the water, Josh sat with his legs hanging over the dock. "OK girls," he started, "here's the story of the poker tournament. He condensed the events to a 20 minute story, the girls listening, intently.

Josh made his Dad the hero, regarding the sprinkler system, and gave most of the credit for surveillance and escorting the players and their entourage, to the others on the team. He was especially proud of Kenyon's role in actually preventing the burglary due to his suspicion of the "accidental drunk" appearing on the blocked out floor.

All in all, he described a team effort, which thwarted "Viper", and upheld the integrity of not only the poker tournament, but also the "Beau Rivage".

At the conclusion, the girls asked a few questions regarding the pros, which they'd seen on TV, and the "loose life" many of them seemed to live.

Josh admitted he couldn't really be accurate about their lifestyle, or off-site antics, but from what he had seen at the tourney they had been relatively normal, if professional poker players could be described as normal.

Connie had a question, "Josh, you said that if one of he entourage had to leave the 'Players' Club', even if for one of the bathrooms, one of your crew accompanied them. Is that right?" Josh answered, "Absolutely, you just can't allow them to have contact with the outside world. They could pass word to someone on playing strategies, who had been playing 'tight, who had been bluffing, who had respect for who, etc."

Connie looked him square into his eyes and asked, "What about the women, Josh? Half Track go with them into the restroom, also?" Josh was stunned. Such an obvious weakness. His real estate sister saw it when he didn't. "I've got to think about that," Josh stammered. "But 90% of the players are men."

Connie, was pressing her point, "Even if that was true, Josh, these people in the Players Club were the friends, families and spouses of the players. Very possibly this group was only 50% male." "So, you were only 50% secure?" Jess asked, taking Connie's side of the argument. "I need to think about this," Josh stalled.

"No you don't," said Connie, "you need a woman on the team. You know, it's not the 1950's anymore. Beaver Cleaver's Mom doesn't exist, anymore."

Josh realized he had a blind spot. Those years in the Marines, all the combat missions in Afghanistan, fighting the Taliban, sometimes hand-to hand. That was all great. But this was not the Marines, or Afghanistan. This was a world with laws, and smart criminals. Criminals of both sexes.

The thinkers, and the instinctive, won the battles. He couldn't lose a client because of his myopia or stereotypes.

"It's something I need to talk through with Kenyon, but I think that Connie brought up an excellent point," he said, to no one except himself.

A Close Call

Monday came to the Flowers' home with all the promise of a beautiful, late fall day in the deep south. Tom, Josh, and Connie were all at work. Josh still had a few days off until his next project, and was using that time to catch up on some reading, and by attending an electronics expo in New Orleans with Milo. His company had to remain state of the art to be successful, and new products or updates were developing very quickly.

Karen was in the midst of preparing her garden for the upcoming wet winter. Most of her harvest had occurred in the late summer/early fall, so she hadn't been gardening every day for the past couple of weeks.

Today was all about turning under dead growth, taking out the last few pumpkins and other late harvest produce, and performing a very thorough weeding project. The less weeds you left behind, the better start you'd get in the spring.

After she finished with that, hopefully by tomorrow, she would clean all her tools, garden implements, gloves, etc., and store them in the shed near the back gate leading to the bay. She was a thorough person who didn't like to start playing "catch-up" when it was time to plant next spring.

Karen was thorough in winterizing her garden. Today she was crawling inside individual portions of her "little farm", as Tom liked to call it, pulling out the last few weeds.

She had begun, several years ago, with only one section behind a chicken wire fence, buried a few inches into the ground, to discourage rabbits and squirrels. It had netting on top of 6 foot stakes which allowed sun and water in, but kept birds out.

Today, she had 4 such sections, each containing crops which had similar needs of sun, water, and fertilizer. The particular area she was in, held the last of the pumpkins. She would collect those, and can them for use in the future.

Karen crawled on all fours to the furthest corner of the garden in order to work her way forward, toward the gate. She envisioned couple of ibuprofen in her future when completed. She turned toward the gate, and only a few feet away she saw something which took her breath away.

A "copperhead", previously sunning itself behind a large pumpkin, now had her full attention. It had slithered directly between Karen and the gate, and was staring directly at her with those cat-like eyes, it's forked tongue flicking the air. The reptile was trying to detect warmth and motion. She was lucky that she hadn't stepped on it, that's how most snake bites occur, just a snake defending itself.

This wasn't any ordinary snake. It was classified as a pit viper by herpetologists, joined by the various rattlesnake types, and water moccasins. This was one of the most poisonous creatures in America. The snake had two hinged fangs in the front of a triangular shaped head, which injected poison into whatever it struck. The results were sometimes fatal. The situation Karen was in, offered the possibility of multiple bites, increasing the mortality rate.

Karen knew if she moved the animal would sense it and strike. She thought about using her straw gardening hat as a shield, which would probably result in her arms and hands taking the brunt of the attack. Karen lifted her eyes without moving, and saw a stealthy yellow creature approaching through the open gate. Goldie had never come into one of the fenced garden areas in the past. She knew it was forbidden. Karen realized that the dog must have sensed a lack of activity, and had come to investigate. Goldie's investigation was complete. She was locked in a frozen position, never taking her eyes off the dangerous intruder.

Goldie went into action. "Whoof, whoof", came repeatedly. Goldie running from side to side, just out of striking range. More loud barking and feinting toward the copperhead drew an attempted strike, just missing the dog. Goldie stayed a moving target, keeping the snake's attention on her, and away from Karen.

It was after what seemed to Karen to be forever, the reptile sensed that it was in danger. Unknown forces on both sides. It quickly retreated, slithering through the fence, heading in the direction of the back fence and the dock. Goldie headed after it. "Goldie, no," screamed Karen. "Goldie, stop, stay."

Goldie obeyed, and stopped about ten feet short of where the snake was still moving at it's top speed toward the fence. The dog turned toward Karen, and walked back to the garden entrance, and lay down outside. "Goldie, come here," Karen called, shakily. She went inside the fenced area, for the second time in her life and put her head on Karen's lap. Her Mom was still shaking, still crying as she caressed her four-legged daughter.

"You've always been here for us," Karen finally said. "And, I guess today was my turn to be rescued. And don't think for a minute that I don't know who you really are."

Karen told Tom the story when he got home from work. Tom just shook his head. "A gift," he said, "A real gift."

Past and Future

They had been sent to relieve a platoon who had observation duty near the Pakistani border. The 3 squads had been in position for a week, and it was time to rotate out. Just like the platoon they were replacing, Josh's group would have 3 observation camps about 500 meters apart, almost a mile of distance, on a hilltop, facing east.

They were to report back to Baghram on the radio, on all Taliban movement. The military was looking to see just who was supplying the enemy from Pakistan, but the brass were very cautious about upsetting our Pakistani "allies", and wanted no border incidents to shake that fragile friendship, if at all possible.

The Black Hawks landed on the west side of the hill, about 500 meters apart, and shielded from the border. The incoming squads deploying up to the ridgeline, passing the relieved squads coming down. Total time on the ground for the aircraft, less than 45 seconds.

Suddenly, mortars and rockets started dropping from the sky onto all 3 positions. AK-47 fire was everywhere. It was a well conceived trap. Someone had tipped off the enemy about the platoon rotation, and they used the time between one platoon going down the west side of the hill, and the replacements getting up the hill to set up attack positions in close proximity. The platoon leader, Captain Hanks, called in the attack to Base Command, asking for air support. They replied with an odd question, "Niner-3, Niner-3. Can you tell which side of the border the enemy fire is coming from? Repeat can you see the origin of the attack?"

Where had that come from?, thought Josh. What did it matter? U.S. Marines were under attack. "I don't care where the attackers are, we need help," replied Hanks.

After about 30 seconds of a heated discussion back at Baghram Control, he heard, "Request denied, Niner-3, repeat, request denied, can't fire at the border, can't take that chance." Hanks was stunned. He had heard stories of troops being abandoned due to politics, in Viet Nam, he just never thought it would happen again.

Hanks bellowed, "Then request immediate extraction, Base command, repeat, request immediate extraction at previous drop off point., about 500 meters west of current position." Base came back, "Request granted, location verified."

It was a deadly retreat, Marines dragging other, wounded or dying Marines behind them. In another few minutes, the platoon had set up defensive positions at the bottom of the hill. There was a small gully, about 3 feet deep, with some rocks on the edge which provided a small amount of cover. The spotter-sniper teams had been the last to gain safety.

"Casualty report," Hanks screamed into the Radio. Josh came back, 1 gone, two injured, one seriously," he replied. Then Nash's squad, "2 gone, 1 minor wound," said Nash. Hanks had 2 dead as well, plus one bad injury, a gut wound. Finally, the 3 Black Hawks arrived.

They carried the dead and wounded onto the choppers. Josh was the last from his squad to get on. Wait, where was Swanson, the new man. Josh scanned the area, every second on the ground endangered everyone. There he was, huddled behind a rock. He was frozen in place, endangering everyone.

"Come on, Marine," Josh yelled. Swanson didn't move. "Thirty seconds, cover me, I'm going to get him." Josh leapt off the chopper and raced to the frozen Marine. Josh grabbed him and pulled and pushed until he got him on board. Josh jumped on the chopper. His men extending their hands, pulling him on board as the Black Hawk zoomed away.

"I'm hit," Josh couldn't believe those words came from his mouth. A searing flame ran up his leg.

Josh bolted upright in the bed. His sheets were drenched with sweat. Finally his breathing and pulse came under control. The "dream"...again. Well, they were becoming less frequent, but he still caught himself rubbing the scar from his hip replacement surgery.

It was only 5:30, but Josh knew any further attempts to sleep would be futile. Besides, he had to clean up a bit, wash the sheets, and tidy the condo. Connie had asked if she could come over for a talk. About what, Josh had no idea. It was Saturday, and he had nothing going on today. If he had, he would have changed his plans. He thought a lot of Connie. He had seen her grow from a wild child to a proud young professional.

At 9, sharp the doorbell rang, and Josh let Connie in. "Coffee? he asked." No, thanks," Connie responded.

Continuing, she said, "I wanted to come over and get your response to an idea I had a couple of weeks ago. The idea really gelled when we were discussing possible limitations that Special Corps had in dealing with potential threats, who happened to be female."

Josh remembered the conversation which he, Jess, and

Connie had when discussing security gaps in the "Journey to the Top" poker tournament only a short time ago.

Part of Special Corps' responsibility was to make sure there were no "leaks" from supporters, friends, and spouses who were watching the tournament on closed circuit TV from a VIP lounge. Once this group was in the lounge they could not make phone calls (cell phones were confiscated) and you had to be escorted to and from the bathroom by one of Josh's staff. The tournament sponsors did not want there to be any chance of privileged information regarding one player's strategy, so far, to be leaked.

Jess and Connie reminded Josh that even though the vast majority of the players were male, the mix of supporters, friends, and spouses, was much closer to 50/50. Josh's people had accompanied the men into the restrooms, but had only waited outside the ladies rooms. There could have been a cell phone planted inside the restroom, or another person who could relay information, waiting for their contact to come in.

"Yeah, I've been thinking about that one, sis," he admitted. "I just don't know where to start. I've been lucky so far, with Kenyon, 'Track', Julio, and of course, Milo."

"I've always been a leader, but I'm not sure I can be a good manager, like Dad. Picking people scares me, but I can see the hole in the organization. Someday, I'll wind up losing a case or a client because of that hole."

He continued, "So what do I do now? Run an ad in the paper? Hire someone from a competitor? Viper is history, and I wouldn't have any of them, anyway. I have no idea," he admitted.

Josh summarized, "The fact is, I need another person, regardless. I use Pete and Drake when I need then, but, they're not always available. We're in the position where I either have to grow or shrink...and I'm not into shrinking."

"That's why I'm here," Connie said. Josh looked puzzled. "Let me explain," Connie said.

"When we were locked out of the casino while delivering Holly, who had the idea and guts to go find Dad?"

"When you wanted Holly to stay on the ground floor, who said she'd be safer upstairs?"

"Who saw the hole in the security and is the hardest working, most honest, and smartest female you know? Plus, is someone you can trust." "The answer to all those is me."

"You, Connie, but what about real estate?" Josh asked. "You've invested time, money, and energy into that, and you've been very successful."

"Josh, the market is dead right now, and my proposal is this. I come to work for Special Corps, full time. You've admitted you need the help in order to be successful. If we have a weekend off, and I want to sell a house, great, but my priority will belong to Special Corps."

"Well, Josh began, we'd have to get you a firearms license, some training, law enforcement classes, and maybe some familiarity with self defense"

"Done, done, and done," Connie exclaimed. I received my gun license two weeks ago, after classes with the State. I finished #1 out of 14 in the class."

She opened her purse and showed Josh a Sig Sauer P239, 9mm. "Bought that last week," she said. "Plus I'm taking the same on-line class you took a couple of years ago, in law enforcement. Lastly, I'm taking mixed martial arts classes two nights a week, and a boxing class every Wednesday," she said.

Josh was blown away. Sometimes he forgot how tenacious and dedicated this young woman was. "What about Mom and Dad? How will they feel about the change?"

"Mom thinks it's a great idea. A little scary, but holding an open house in the wrong part of town can be just as dangerous. And Dad, I haven't spoken to him yet, but when has he been anything but supportive?"

Josh rubbed his chin. "The timing is good. We have a couple of smaller jobs this month, then a real doozy, next month, which we'll have to prepare for and be fully operational to handle." Josh finished, "Well, you know I have to talk to Kenyon about it. It's my company, but he's got 'sweat equity', and a piece of ownership coming. I can't leave him out of the decision."

Connie beamed, "He's fine with it. In fact he encouraged me, it was partly his idea. And Jess says it makes sense in lots of ways."

Josh was stunned again, but decided to have fun with it, "Have you gotten your first raise yet? I'd just like to know," he laughed. "OK," he concluded, "we'll work out the details later. But, not a word to anyone else until I have time to talk to the rest of my crew."

Jess gave him a big hug. "You know I'll never let you down, Josh. I'll be the hardest working person you have."

"No, Connie, your work ethic has never been questioned by anyone I know. But hard work in this business is no guarantee of success. Being smart, alert, and sometimes even thinking a little like a criminal, usually gets the job done."

Josh finished, "That's why I know this will be a success. You're a natural born conspirator." They both laughed over that.

Connie turned to leave and waved, "I'll see you at dinner tomorrow, and in the office at 8 am on Monday."

Doris, Here & There

Today was Sunday. Josh and Connie had agreed to meet at the Flowers' home at 10:30, in order to break the news to Dad about Connie joining Special Corps. They shouldn't have tried.

"I already know," Tom Flowers said. "Your mother talked to me last night. Why am I always the last to know?" he asked looking up into the ceiling.

"Well Dad, if it's any consolation, I was the second-to-last to find out, and it's my company," Josh replied.

"Well," Tom conceded, "she'll be a real asset to you. I deal with over 300 employees, there are very few I can turn my back on. You won't have any trust issues, and that's 50% of my job."

With that out of the way, Josh and his sisters had some precious time to spend together, along with Goldie, in the back yard and down by the water. Jess told her brother about the close call Karen had with the copperhead, in the garden, and how Goldie had intervened, and saved the day in yet another family crisis.

They walked up to the house, right at noon, awaiting the arrival of Grandma Doris and Max. Karen had told them the plan of action. Karen had reached out to some AA experts, and wanted to use her position to exhibit some "tough love."

This concept would work, as long as Doris realized that there wasn't a weak link she could turn to, who would enable her to continue her drunken lifestyle.

Karen knew she must have a long talk with Max, as he would be the one who would most bear the brunt of Doris' calls for help. But, after all, Max was the one who had come to her, asking for help.

Max and Doris arrived just past noon. Doris was tense and edgy. She may have remembered the previous weekend, and how she had left, the rest of the family eating while she was passed out on the porch. Karen doubted that Doris had been drinking less, but her arrival at the Flowers home today was the most sober she had witnessed in months.

Grandma Doris had sat on the sofa and exchanged small talk for a few minutes, when she excused herself to the bathroom, Karen noticed that she took her purse with her. She knew what that meant. Karen took the opportunity to wave Max into the kitchen for a talk, but told Jess and Connie to stay there too. It would seem less conspiratorial that way.

"How's she doing, Max?" Karen asked. "Not great," Max admitted. "She probably thinks we're all against her." Karen replied, "Max, you have to be tough, hang in there. I'm not saying pour all the liquor down the drain, even though that's probably what she needs, but tell her how much you appreciate her struggle."

"Tell her you care more for her when she's there, not when she's passed out in some drunken stupor."

Predictably, Doris came out of the bathroom, certain that she was the object of discussion among the family. She made a "beeline" toward the kitchen, and rounding the corner said, "So you're all in here talking about me!"

Connie and Jess were preparing the lobsters which had just been put into the kettle. Karen was filling glasses with iced tea, and Max was taste testing the vegetable medley to make sure it was prepared "al dente."

"Excuse me," Karen asked. "We're preparing dinner, do you want to contribute Mom?" Karen asked.

"No, Doris replied, "I was missing Max, and wanted to make sure he was OK."

Right, Karen thought, but everything was going according to plan. Max was protected, Doris had been shown that she was not the center of attention, or conversation. Karen had learned through her AA contacts, that part of the problem was an addiction to attention. Thinking that you were the most important part of the family unit could only be solidified when you cried out for attention.

Karen was concerned about the contents of her Mom's purse. She was certain there was a bottle in there, but she decided to try to address the entire situation one small step at a time. Searching her purse could send Doris off the deep end. She was making progress, the purse would have to wait.

The dinner was superb. Lobster was one of those items which had a very slim margin for error in it's preparation. Being a shellfish, you certainly didn't want to serve it, underdone. On the other hand, a minute or two extra cooking could produce a stiff, rubbery meal, fit for no one.

Jess regretted that she had not taken a quick, on-line, trip to Boston's "Legal Seafood", the national expert on food from that area. However, she had treated the crustacean as a large crawfish (same family, right?), and had never gone wrong.

The dinner was "5-Star", Emeril LaGasse could not have done better. Doris had stayed (almost) sober throughout the meal and seemed to enjoy her food, and the concurrent conversation, more than any Sunday in recent memory.

Tom commented, "Cooking this good, and a future pit boss too. It's too good to be true." Jess looked up. They had never discussed the incident involving the stubborn shooter and the dice.

Tom continued, "Timmy Roland told me the story. He was so proud of you, it was like you were his daughter. And, he doesn't pass out compliments easily. If he was impressed, then I'm impressed too. Good job, Jess." "Thanks Dad, I appreciate that," Jess replied while blushing.

They finished off the dinner with Josh's favorite dessert, pecan pie.

After the great meal, Josh collected the trash for the outside containers. Didn't want shellfish smelling up the place. As he removed the lobster bag they'd brought from the fish market, Josh smiled as he looked at the tag. It read, "TVM Seafood Co., Tran Van Minh, son and daughter, proprietors." There were now 7 boats on the label. Some things in life are worth taking a chance on, Josh thought back, 'You take check from me today? I get cashiers check tomorrow?'

Josh wiped a bit of irritant from his eye, went back inside and collected his sisters, walking back down to the small dock with Goldie trailing along. Josh looked at the two year old Lab and said, "Sounds like you came through for Mom in the clutch, girl." Goldie just wagged her tail and cut playfully back and forth between the three of them. She was herding them just like a good sheepdog.

Connie repeated Karen's perspective on Goldie. "You know Josh, Mom thinks she the old Goldie who's been reincarnated. There are big similarities and coincidences."

Josh responded, "Well, the copperhead experience probably cemented that opinion in her head. She has always had her suspicions about how this one mysteriously showed up, but who knows? There are loads of unexplained things in the world."

"Yeah, like Max," Jess kidded, and they broke out in laughter. Goldie celebrated the jovial mood by doing her jumping routine, thankfully the bank was dry, so she left no muddy footprints on her "victims".

While the "kids" were outside Karen and Tom were talking with Doris and Max. They talked about Tom's job, the girls, Goldie's heroics...anything but grandma's drinking problem. Karen thought that since she was more sober than usual, Doris would appreciate being included in the family discussion.

She had been told that treating Doris more like an adult, and less like a child who had to be monitored, could help with her self-esteem. It was worth a try.

In Karen's eyes, things were progressing, nicely. But, she also knew from her AA contacts, that there would usually be at least two or three more lapses in the recovery program.

People like Doris were users. The first time they realized that they were no longer the center of attention, they would exhibit behavior which demanded the focus and worry of the entire family.

As the discussion waned, Max and Doris said their goodbyes, and headed to the Senior Center.

"One day at a time," Karen said. "Yep," Tom agreed. "That's all we can do."

The Plan

At 8 am, Special Corps had a meeting at their little office just off of Popp's Ferry Road. Milo was at his desk, as usual, Julio and Kenyon on the sofa, Half Track was sitting on the second desk in the room, and the desk was straining with his 300+ pounds on it.

They had all met Connie from time to time either at events, or when Josh held his summer barbeque cookout.

Josh waited until the early morning banter died down, to begin the discussion. Kenyon knew what was coming, but the others didn't. Everyone knew that Josh wasn't a "meeting" type of boss. He was a planner and a doer, so something must be up.

Josh began, "I've got some good news for everyone," he said. "I've done a lot of thinking the past couple of months about the direction we should be moving in. Even though the next two weeks are going to be slow, after that we are slammed...booked solid through the holidays," Josh said.

"I'm not complaining," he said, "but that puts us in an uncomfortable position. Either we turn business down, which I don't want to do, or we will be stretched too thin, and that's when mistakes happen, and people get hurt."

"Now that 'Viper' is out of business, I think the demand will go up for our services, and we can't always depend on Pete and Drake to be available, they're busier also," he said.

"We either have to grow larger and smarter, or some new competitor will come in and take up the slack, and we'll go back to fighting for business like we did in the beginning."

"Kenyon and I have discussed this a few times, and we're of the same mind on expansion. Also, that poker tournament opened my eyes to something we're missing.

"We accompanied all the men from the men from the 'Player's Club' into the restroom. But, he continued, we waited outside the restrooms for the women. One of them could have blown the whole thing apart, and we wouldn't get the job next year." Julio started nodding, along with Milo and "Track." They got the picture, loud and clear.

"We need a woman on the team. We've been missing that in Special Corps. In this room, I'm honored to be among people who were some of the best combat veterans who ever represented this country. And yes, Milo, I'm proud to have you as a team member, as well."

"And that's what I'm getting at. Milo doesn't think like me, or Julio. He fills a very important role in this organization because he thinks like a computer expert. We didn't need another combat veteran when he was hired, we needed someone good with computers."

"So, by now you've all figured out why Connie is here. We need to fill a big hole in Special Corps. But we're not bringing her on board because she's my sister."

"I want her here "despite" the fact that she's my sister. She's always thought that she is smarter than me, and maybe she is. But she will give us access to places we can't go now, and she'll bring a fresh perspective in evaluating situations which occur, and in operational planning."

"In preparation for this move she's taken the State firearms classes and has a 'carry' permit, along with a Sig P239."

"She's almost finished with her on-line law enforcement certification, and is taking self defense classes three nights a week. One thing which I can promise you is, she won't be a burden."

"I can also promise you that she'll get no special treatment because of our relationship. She'll be an equal part of the team, no more, no less."

Josh finished. "I'm done. We've got a couple of weeks with only small jobs, until we get really busy. Does anyone have any questions, comments or concerns? Bring them up now, or keep them to yourselves for good."

Josh got a little round of applause. The guys knew that this wasn't his thing. Half Track came over and gave Connie a hug, which almost cracked the girl's ribs.

"If I can, I've got three things to say," Connie stated. "One, I really look forward to being part of this very special team."

"Two, I am smarter than Josh."

"And lastly, can you guys remember to put the toilet seat down in the bathroom?"

Hoots and howls followed her remarks.

A Trip West

Connie and Jess had been to Los Angeles this past May, invited by none other than Holly Santa Cruz. They had assisted her in the spring, when she was fleeing her estranged husband (now ex-husband). Holly had repaid them with a big check, and invited the girls to witness the making of Holly's newest music video. The title song was appropriately named "*Runaway Fever*".

It was an instant #1 hit. They say that athletes are superstitious, baseball players not washing their socks while they're on a big hitting streak, football teams eating the identical pre-game meal during a winning stretch, etc. Entertainers are worse. And this was going to work to Jess and Connie's advantage. They were up to the challenge.

After the smash hit of "*Runaway Fever*", Holly wanted the girls to be at the filming of her newest music video. To her, the girls were good luck charms, and this move was also a way to repay those who had helped her a few months back. It was due to start shooting next week.

Obviously, the girls had nothing to do with the music video's past success, but Holly wasn't taking any chances. They would stay behind the scenes at the shoot, but just being there was a special treat.

They had both taken the week off from work, it was a slow time in the casino and for Special Corps. In fact, Josh had two empty weeks to fill before the rush of the Holiday season began. He had agreed to drive the girls to the airport where, as before, Holly's Learjet would pick the girls up Sunday morning and deliver them back 4 days later.

Sunday finally arrived, Josh got to the Flowers' home at 8:30. As he pulled up, he saw Kenyon's Ford Explorer sitting outside. Josh went inside and Kenyon was drinking coffee with the girls and Tom.

Josh's puzzled look allowed Kenyon to explain. Kenyon said "I wanted to talk to you about a couple of ideas I have. And so when Connie told me you were taking them to the airport, I thought I'd tag along and we could talk on the way back."

"It's nothing urgent, just a couple of ideas I have to go after a different category of client. In other words, more money for the company."

Josh was all for that and looked forward to hearing what his friend, and associate, had to say.

"Fine by me," Josh said. "You girls ready?" Were they ever! On the way out to Josh's Range Rover Kenyon stopped and grabbed an envelope out of his SUV. Then he hopped in the "shotgun" position and they were off on the 20 minute ride to the airport.

Josh felt the girl's excitement growing as they took the Airport Road exit. They pulled up in front of the terminal for private planes and could even see Holly's plane on the ground, less than 100 yards away, with the distinctive HSC logo on the side. The plane was a bright, silvery bird, built more like a missile, than an airplane.

The girls jumped out, grabbed their bags, and waited. What are they waiting for, Josh wondered.

Kenyon looked at Josh, and held out his open hand.

"Your gun and your keys, right now," Kenyon said. Josh was flabbergasted "What are you talking about?" asked Josh with surprise. He wasn't going anywhere.

"Connie was right, she is smarter than you," Kenyon laughed. "You're going with them," he explained. "Now if I were you, I wouldn't keep the lady waiting."

Josh turned back to the plane, and there was Holly Santa Cruz, standing beside the bottom step of the Lear Jet's entrance. Copper shaded hair, green, flashing eyes, wearing a black, skin-tight, outfit, waving hello.

"And," Kenyon added, "here's $2,000 out of petty cash," handing the envelope to Josh. "You might need some new clothes. See you in a few days."

Josh thought back about the "rain check", and handed his friend the Range Rover keys and his Glock, and walked arm in arm with his sisters to the plane.

Biloxi...A Special Place

During Biloxi's long history, eight flags have flown over her. These flags included the flags of six countries: France, England, Spain, the Republic of West Florida, The Confederate States of America, and the United States stars and stripes. The other two flags were state flags: the Magnolia State Flag and the current Mississippi State Flag.

Pierre Le Moyne, Sieur d'Iberville (after whom the Biloxi's Back Bay region is named) founded Biloxi. Landing onto what is a group of barrier islands collectively known as the Mississippi sound, on February 10, 1699. On February 13, De'Iberville and 14 men landed at present-day Biloxi. After several days the French became friends with the Biloxi Indians, which is still the name of the Biloxi High School athletic teams today.

The Spanish and French influence survive throughout the region. They still celebrate Mardi Gras, and the other Christian holidays. The predominant religion of the local, non-military, population is Catholic. But the community is truly multi-denominational, with a large Jewish population.

Biloxi was the retirement home of Jefferson Davis, President of the Confederacy. Mr. Davis' home, still existing along the beach on highway 90, is named "Beauvoir" or beautiful view, in French. He lived there from 1877 – 1889, along with his dog "Traveler" named after the famous horse of Robert E. Lee.

The evolution of Biloxi involved the warm Gulf waters, abundant with life. Around the turn of the 20th century, Biloxi was widely regarded as the seafood capital of the world. Dozens of shrimp and fishing boats found sea life plentiful. In the 1920's Biloxi had over 50 active seafood factories and processing plants.

Some of the first fishermen were Austrians from the Dalmatia Coast.

From 1890 to 1910, Bohemians, Czechs, Greeks, and Croatians were some of the first foreign laborers.

Cajun families had been a strong base in the region for decades, arriving from Louisiana. Today, Vietnamese make up a large portion of the seafood industry.

Keesler Air Force Base was activated in 1941. It has served many functions, but has always focused on training. From B-24s to Aerospace Projects.

The tourist industry boomed in the 1950s when Biloxi and adjacent cities imported white sand and created it's "largest in the world" (at that time) man made beach, which stretched for 27 miles. Illegal gambling was also pervasive in the 50's and 60's.

Of course, bars and night clubs had flourished in Biloxi for decades before, serving liquor, and live entertainment (in fact, in 1967, Jayne Mansfield died the night of an appearance at a local night club in Biloxi), and you could buy beer and wine in many convenience stores. All you had to do was to pay a fee to the state to look the other way, and they did. With the legalization of casino gaming in the early 1990s, Biloxi was suddenly transformed into a destination spot for short or long vacations. Casinos and their peripheral supports of hotels and restaurants grew almost overnight.

Biloxi has been hit by numerous hurricanes, the largest and most intense, was Camille, in August 1969. It remains the most powerful storm to make landfall in the U.S., with winds of up to 220 m.p.h. But, they rebuilt.

On August 29, 2005, Hurricane Katrina hit the Mississippi Gulf Coast with high winds, heavy rains and a 27-foot storm surge, causing massive damage to the area. Katrina came ashore during the high tide of +2.3 feet at 6:56AM,

Two days later, in an interview on MSNBC, Governor Barbour stated that 90% of the buildings along the coast in Biloxi and neighboring Gulfport had been destroyed by the hurricane.

Several of the casinos, including the "Beau Rivage", and "Hard Rock" were devastated, some torn off their foundations and thrown into the coastal buildings, contributing to the damage.

The local population rebuilt again. With New Orleans getting all the attention, the people of the Mississippi Gulf Coast had 95% of the infrastructure and businesses restored within 3 years. Schools, libraries, and churches got priority. Roadways were redone, bridges repaired, "Beauvoir" restored.

The casinos and hotels were quickly rebuilt, over 50 casinos exist today. Anyone who wanted a job, had 2 or 3 to choose from, and many people on the coast were taking more than 1. Just as after Camille in 69, the spirit of this diverse community was a shining example of American pride.

They did it themselves, again. And they will the next time too, as well. This is a proud part of the our country.